Finding My Heart

A Summer Shores Novella

Rachel Blanchard

ISBN: 978-1-7376719-2-3 (Paperback)

978-1-7376719-3-0 (E-Book)

Cover Design by Sofia Constantino

A Note to the Reader

Although it can be read as a standalone romance, this companion novella is set between the final chapter and the epilogue of *First in My Heart*, the first installment in the Summer Shores series.

1

Kaleigh ran her fingers through her auburn hair, content to sacrifice a put-together ponytail for an ounce more patience.

"Mom," she said levelly, "You know I can't call out of any more shifts."

Lana picked at her hot pink talons, not looking her daughter in the eye. "What I know is you told me I wouldn't turn into Aaron's full-time babysitter."

Kaleigh released a shaky exhale. "It won't always be like this. I'm so close to saving enough money."

Lana rolled her eyes. "This again. How will you pass college classes when you can't even handle a retail job?"

Kaleigh considered citing the numbers she'd crunched—how much more her annual income would be after investing in her education. But she knew it was pointless. And a nagging, heart-sickening part of her felt that Lana had made a good point.

It was a struggle to hold down her job and not totally ignore Aaron. She did her best, but still came home to a boy who grew taller and smarter each day she was away. *Soon you'll have flexible work hours and more time off,* Kaleigh chanted to herself.

She kept her voice calm. "Can you please help me out Saturday, so I don't have to call out?"

"I'm sorry, but I'm already watching him tomorrow. I can't cancel on the girls again, or they'll stop asking me to go out."

Like Kaleigh didn't know how that felt. How it hurt when every friend she thought had cared about her couldn't bother to keep calling once things got hard.

They'd thought it was cool enough to be tight with the pregnant girl, to ask questions about her appointments and symptoms in algebra class. But when the baby had arrived, after the cute hospital pics had been taken and the long nights set in, it wasn't as fun to be Kaleigh's friend.

Kaleigh wished Lana could brush it off the way that she did, but that would never happen. The admiration of others made Lana's world go round. Well, Aaron was Kaleigh's world. She would be there for him somehow.

"All right, I'll try and make it work."

"That's my girl." Lana patted Kaleigh on the cheek.

"Mommy?" Aaron emerged from the bedroom he and Kaleigh shared, his fire truck in hand. He ran to Kaleigh, and she gathered him into her arms.

She kissed his tawny head. "Hey, baby."

"I'm not a baby." Aaron jutted his chin out.

"You'll always be my baby," Kaleigh told him, even as he broke her grip and wiggled down to the floor.

"Do you want to see the pictures I drew today?" he asked, tugging her to their room.

"Of course!"

The times that Kaleigh got home from work and saw Aaron were the lightest, sweetest parts of her days. She tried her best then to shed the iron mantle of worry and devote all her attention and love to him. However, she often found herself so drained from the day that her thoughts strayed back to her hefty to-do list and complete lack of options.

Doggedly, Kaleigh forced herself back to the present—to rectangles scrawled in red crayon, dotted with superhero stickers.

"You did a wonderful job," she said, and Aaron's hazel eyes glistened.

The urge to give him everything she could was overwhelming, and it put a fire back under the hopes that her mother's discouragement had extinguished. They could get their own place.

They could have a better life. Aaron deserved a mom who would at least work toward that. Kaleigh'd convince her boss to give her another chance. And, eventually, she'd get a job that could provide them with a real future.

Smoothing Aaron's bangs back from his bronzed forehead, she imagined all the precious minutes she would gain back with her big boy when all of her dreams came true.

* * *

"I hate to do this, Kaleigh." Her manager's usually warm expression was doused in a mask of professionalism.

"Then don't."

Jenny said, "I want to help you, but at the end of the day, I have to follow procedure."

"Please, just give me more time to figure something out." Kaleigh's hands clasped together. She wasn't above begging.

"Look, I appreciate your honesty, and I hope that you do figure something out. But if you call out one more time, you'll to have to find another job."

"Is it really calling out when I give you a day's notice?"

"It is when we're short-staffed and there's not anyone to take your place. My hands are tied."

"I'll take her shift." The door leading out to Hydrangea's stockroom had opened to reveal none other than Jackson Green. He strolled in and leaned against a rack of girls' t-shirts.

Great, Kaleigh thought. *Him again.*

"Sorry to interrupt," Jackson continued, "but I was on break and happened to overhear your conversation."

Right. The man had more likely been pacing the hall like a mangy cat, waiting to pounce the moment Kaleigh was free.

Jenny dropped the stack of papers—presumably containing Kaleigh's spotty attendance record—that she had been surreptitiously rearranging during their uncomfortable conversation.

"Are you sure?" their boss asked Jackson. "You've already worked six days this week."

"Afraid of paying me more overtime?" He winked—which Kaleigh thought was inappropriate. She worried his smarminess might bring her breakfast back up, but Jenny just looked relieved.

"No, that's something that I can arrange. Kaleigh, you're off the hook." She leaned over and eyed Kaleigh significantly. "For now."

"Thank you." Kaleigh rose to escape the suffocating room.

Jackson followed close behind, but Kaleigh didn't look back. Instead, she barked over her shoulder at him, "Why did you do that?"

"You're welcome," he replied, evidently used to her ice-princess treatment.

"I know you don't need the money." Kaleigh threw her cream-colored locker door open. She never could wrap her head around the fact that some people came to a job for an experience, or to kill time, instead of for survival.

Even though he had done her a favor, Jackson's privilege coupled with his attitude would never gain her admiration. "So, are you trying to go out with me again, or do you actually feel guilty about being a player and you're thinking you can make up for it?"

"Could it be possible that I cared you were in trouble and wanted to help you?" Jackson asked.

"No, I don't think that could be possible."

Jackson's heavy sigh made Kaleigh turn around. "Will you ever stop thinking the worst of me?" he asked.

"See? You are thinking about yourself!"

Jackson's shoulders slumped, but it was probably just an act. Still—though he didn't need to know how much—he had come through for her. "But thanks anyway."

His face brightened, making Kaleigh regret giving him any encouragement. She grabbed her tote, slammed the locker door shut, and hurried home.

* * *

Left in Kaleigh's wake again, Jackson leaned back against the lockers.

It was clear she thought he wanted a challenge and was only after her because she turned him down. But the truth was, Jackson tended to bolt when things got hard, not dig in his heels and stay.

He couldn't argue that he wanted to take Kaleigh out again. She was a firecracker—albeit a short firecracker. Jackson smiled at the memory of her head cocked up at him in defiance. She had an athlete's compact build, long, dark red hair, and eyes the color of a tempestuous sea.

But his attraction ran deeper than the surface. Beneath Kaleigh's eyes lay a rock-solid strength. A fighting spirit powered her trim arms, a determination to work like none he'd seen before, whether she swiftly unloaded boxes for inventory, or slowed down to count pennies with a kid at the register. Kaleigh was an intense force of nature that was rapidly sweeping him in.

He'd been careless when they first met. Initially, their interactions were harmless. He'd been avoiding a confrontation with Ava—the coworker he wasn't sure he still wanted to date—but there were plenty of shifts when Ava wasn't there and he and Kaleigh got a chance to talk. They bonded over reality television and pop music. Over lunch one day, he'd convinced her to take a walk with him to a nearby nature reserve.

Something about the lofty pines and the hush of the forest trail created an atmosphere of enchantment, removing Kaleigh's typical hesitation.

They spoke of crazy dreams, of climbing mountains in Costa Rica and seeing the Cliffs of Moher in Ireland. Jackson hadn't mentioned he was taking steps to travel to Costa Rica back then. He'd been too captivated by the gleam of fantasy in Kaleigh's eyes.

Then, Ava appeared at the wrong time. Kaleigh blew up, and her initial hesitation was replaced with hatred. Usually Jackson would shake it off, knowing there'd be another girl around the corner. Now, he had the sense that there wouldn't ever be another girl like Kaleigh.

She was nothing like Jackson. It was obvious that she was better than him. But maybe that was just what he needed. He couldn't help but feel that Kaleigh was a key piece of the puzzle he kept trying to assemble into a significant life.

His yearlong term as a humanitarian volunteer in Costa Rica would be the starting point, but wouldn't it be nice to have someone there for him once he came back?

First things first, Jackson told himself. *You've got to get her to give you the time of day.*

His coworkers' conversations floated closer through the door which opened up to the main floor, calling him back to the present. With one elbow, Jackson pushed himself off of the lockers and strolled out like a man who had a clue what he was doing.

* * *

Having a Sunday morning off after working seven shifts straight made Jackson want to pull his duvet over his head to block out the sunlight. However, the same discipline that led him to lift weights every day since he was fourteen made him roll over and climb out of bed.

It wasn't that he was such an established churchgoer now. He showed up, didn't know the tunes to any of the songs, and was typically clueless as to what Bible story the pastor referenced. Still, Jackson had decided to try something, and he figured he ought to do it right. The people who went there had a closeness, a contentment that he needed. Badly.

Jackson's Siberian husky followed his owner out of bed and to the door, his tail swinging like a high-speed metronome. After leashing Duke and donning his slippers, Jackson walked the dog through the hall, down the elevator, and to the lawn in his red silk pajama pants.

The sleepwear had been a surprisingly welcome Christmas present from his parents' professional shopper, but still, his state of undress left Jackson grateful that the other residents in his building rarely saw fit to wake up before ten on the weekend.

The upside of nine in the morning was its stiff breeze which cut the summer heat. The clouds rolling in gave the sky a mismatched appearance of gray storm and golden sun. Usually, the Florida rain held off until the afternoon, but by the looks of it, Jackson would need to take his umbrella to church.

When Duke finished his business, Jackson took him inside. Jackson shed his pjs, which were peppered with white hairs, then poured Duke fresh water and chow to encourage him to keep his distance from today's outfit.

Back in his walk-in closet, Jackson chose a crisp aqua button-up and gray linen pants, completing the ensemble with leather Oxfords. Then he set to work flattening his rumpled hair, wetting the inky black mess, and gelling it back. As a final touch, he spritzed on a designer cologne that he hoped would make him smell like a wooded forest in this Florida swamp.

After chugging down a quick protein-shake breakfast and wincing at the powdery aftertaste, Jackson strode to the entryway. He paused when he reached the hook that held his car key.

Jackson pictured how, once outside, he would reach for the car handle, swing the door open, put his foot in, slide into the seat, press the start button, and lay his hands on the wheel.

He saw headlights, heard brakes squeal, felt a rocking motion and the pelting of dozens of tiny shards of glass.

Jackson shook his head clear of the vivid memories, feeling sweat trail down his neck and temples.

No use ruining a perfectly good shirt, he thought. He would try and drive himself tomorrow.

A quick call, and D'Angelo was on his way to take Jackson to church.

D'Angelo's Italian last name had served as a good omen back when Jackson hired staff to help him in his new home. The driver's ready smile and deep laugh reminded Jackson of his nonna.

Jackson locked up his apartment as a text came in from his dad. He swiped the notification away. No need to deal with that now.

Unlike Jackson's nonna, his father, Marcus, thought that being family-oriented meant cloning his son into himself and having the said offspring make lots of money.

Not that making money was bad. Jackson grinned as he exited the lobby and saw D' Angelo pull his green sports car out front.

Jackson wasn't ready to drive yet, but the black leather passenger seat was comfortably free from responsibility.

"D'Angelo," he said as he eased his way into the car.

"Sir."

"I told you to knock that 'sir' stuff off," Jackson said, cranking up the AC for his side. "You don't beat a man in a game of pool every Saturday night and then turn around and call him 'sir.'"

"I'm sorry, sir. Jackson," D'Angelo corrected himself, a smile tickling his thick mustache.

He was a friendly kind of guy. "D'Angelo. Why didn't you ever get married?"

"I'd like to know the answer to that question myself." He chuckled. "The dating world is not so easy."

"You can say that again." Jackson shook his head.

"Now Mr. Green. You're too young to sound so pessimistic. I'm sure you have no problem finding young ladies to take out."

"Usually." Jackson frowned, and D'Angelo didn't pry. Jackson almost wished he would have, but the man kept up his keen sense of respect—a barrier that Jackson kept trying to break down in fits of loneliness.

"I'm going to set you up with Miss Lewis," Jackson announced.

"Your housekeeper?"

"I know she comes off a little strong, but deep down, I know she's got a heart of gold just waiting to be romanced." Jackson laughed, visualizing D'Angelo in a tailcoat, taking the stern-faced lady by the arm to a dancing class. *Yes, that could work,* Jackson thought.

Miss Lewis did not share D'Angelo's qualms about shouting at her employer when Jackson would leave one too many pairs of shorts on the floor. But she took good care of his place, and sometimes inquired about his hometown, his job, or if there was anything he needed.

Jackson figured she had noticed how he didn't invite any young people over anymore. Instead, he preferred to limp around the apartment with his stupid leg brace like a living shadow.

The road transformed from pavement to a snappy red brick as they got closer to downtown and Summer Shores Church.

"You want to come in?" Jackson asked as they pulled in the parking lot.

"No, thanks. I'll go get a cup of coffee if you don't mind."

"Of course. I'll see you around 12:30?"

"Yes s—" D'Angelo choked off the "sir" this time.

Jackson lifted his hand up in farewell and walked to the church's entrance in the shadow of a grand live oak tree. Once inside, he took a right towards the sanctuary. His eyes scanned the room and found Isaac, a tall man in the back row, who held his curly-headed son while his wife pulled books and toys out of her backpack.

When Jackson needed someone to sit with, Isaac was always the best candidate. Jackson didn't know many people here yet, and, although his ex-coworker Ava Keller always had a wave for him, her new boyfriend Pete's forced smile proved that Jackson was wise to keep his distance.

Jackson could understand Pete's hostility. Jackson regretted how he ended his relationship with Ava. The old Jackson hadn't cared much about hurt feelings and burnt bridges.

He could only prove with time that the accident he had two

months ago battered him on both the outside and inside, forcing him to evaluate, on what was almost his dying day, how few meaningful connections he really had.

"How are you doing, man?" Isaac asked.

"Can't complain." One side of Jackson's mouth twitched up in amusement. He shouldn't complain, but complaints seemed to be the overwhelming theme of his thoughts these days.

"Something on your mind?"

"Someone."

"Is she pretty?"

"Gorgeous. And, not interested."

"That's rough, man."

Jackson laid his head back to rest on his chair's rough green fabric. "I keep trying to think of ways to let her know I'm serious about her. I leave a gift and she tosses it away. I help her at work, I beg for her to listen to me, and still, she can barely stand the sight of me."

"That bad, huh? Sounds frustrating."

"It's driving me crazy. I don't know what else to do except give up."

Isaac pulled the squirming tyke from off his lap and deposited him onto his own seat. "Try not to let it get to you. Some people just need a little more time." He opened his copper-colored Bible to a book labeled Proverbs and quoted, "A soft tongue turneth away wrath."

"Who said that?" Jackson asked.

"King Solomon."

"Yeah, well, King Solomon never met Kaleigh."

2

On her phone at the park, Kaleigh opened up an application to the Physical Therapist Assistant program at Harris Tech—the school she had found to be the most affordable, with virtual class options.

The online application listed a Dr. Reynolds at Summer Shores Hospital among the approved supervisors. Dr. Reynolds would be able to assist Kaleigh as she earned her prerequisite ten observation hours.

As she double-tapped the hospital's phone number to dial it, her thumb twitched slightly. This program would take her one step closer to her dream.

After Kaleigh typed in the right extension, Dr. Reynolds' receptionist answered. The receptionist was able to schedule Kaleigh's first volunteer hour for this Thursday afternoon, after her morning shift at Hydrangea. Kaleigh let out a breath. *So far, so good.*

Kaleigh texted Lana soon after, making sure to mention that it would only be an extra hour of babysitting over the next few weeks. She also thanked her profusely for the help, knowing that Lana would not be thrilled at the additional obligation. Staring at the screen as she anticipated Lana's response, Kaleigh noticed the time at the top turn to one p.m. *Already?*

She glanced up. Aaron met her gaze, waved at her, and continued to climb up the play structure's rock wall. But he had played for an hour already in the heat, and he wasn't sprinting up quite as fast as usual. "Five more minutes, baby," she called, and he nodded.

Confirming her observations, Aaron's limbs seemed heavy when he trudged to the car. He passed out in his booster seat on the way home. Kaleigh smiled at him in the rearview mirror and parked the car in front of their apartment.

That's weird, she thought, noticing that Lana's maroon junker wasn't in the adjacent space. She wondered why her mother hadn't mentioned this morning that she was going out.

Outside, Kaleigh slung her backpack over her right shoulder and positioned her sleeping son over her left. A little snore escaped his puckered lips, and she chuckled. She locked up the car, then keyed into their dark apartment.

Kaleigh opened the living room blinds, since sunshine illuminated the living room much better than the dingy floral lamp she had picked up at a yard sale. As she gently lowered Aaron to the couch, a folded piece of printer paper on the coffee table caught her eye. The fold was too crisp to be Aaron's handiwork.

She opened it up to read Lana's scrawled words:

Kaleigh,

I've found a man who will take good care of me, and I'm moving in with him. I know that sounds bad, but I have always taught you to be responsible for yourself. I hope that you can show your son how to take charge and make life work for you.

—Mom

Kaleigh dropped the note like it had caught fire and watched the paper flutter to the carpet. Running away to live with some new loser was her mom's idea of setting an example?

As if Lana hadn't already taught Kaleigh independence as a kid, when Kaleigh had to forge signatures on her school permission slips or ask a friend's mom to pay for her soccer uniform.

No, Lana was never there for her in all the ways she needed. But at least, when they pooled together their meager resources, Kaleigh had a small degree of relief. If she was counting pennies with Lana's beauty business earnings going toward the rent, and if Kaleigh was unable to pick up overtime hours with Lana's occasional, reluctant babysitting, how were she and Aaron going to survive now?

Kaleigh felt thick walls of hopelessness close in. Her breath hitched in panic. *How could she do this to us?*

Aaron stirred on the couch, and Kaleigh snatched the note back up from the floor. She crumpled it into a ball and threw it in the garbage, then collapsed in a kitchen chair. Collapsed like all her plans for the future just had.

Aaron's sleeping form rustled again, and Kaleigh sat up. *No, there's no time to waste,* she thought. She hunched over the table and scrolled frantically through her phone's contacts, though the short list of names would surely confirm what she already knew—she was alone.

She swiped right past Jackson's number. *Not going there again.* Then she texted Mariana Reyes, who'd been nice enough to trade shifts with her before at work. But, after a moment, Mariana's disappointing response came through. She was going on a beach trip with her family this week.

"Mommy?" Aaron called.

Kaleigh locked her phone and looked up, thinking, *I'll come up with someone by Thursday.* "Yes, sweetie?"

"Where's Grandma?"

Her pulse jumped. "Grandma decided that she wants a bigger place to stay, so she moved out. Now you can have her room all to yourself, if you'd like."

"No thanks. I'd have bad dreams if I didn't sleep with you."

"All right, then. Maybe we'll make the extra bedroom into a playroom."

He didn't seem enthused. "Does Grandma want to live somewhere else because she's tired of watching me?" he asked.

Horrified that Aaron had seemed to pick up on Lana's oft-repeated grievances, Kaleigh leapt up and wrapped her arms around her boy. "No, baby. This isn't because of you. Grandma has a hard time knowing what things are important sometimes." She pulled away to stare into his eyes. "But that has nothing to do with you."

Aaron nodded, but his silence frightened Kaleigh. He took leaving too well for such a little boy. She wished that she could play the roles of father, grandmother, and friend so completely that he would never doubt how much he was loved, and never feel as if he were missing out, but there was only so much of her to go around. And that truth left her feeling wholly inadequate.

Regardless, Kaleigh pasted on a radiant smile. "How about some ice cream?"

That got through to him. Aaron's face lit up. "Before lunch? Really?"

She pulled a carton of orange sherbet out of the freezer. "We sweat a lot at the park. I think we deserve it, don't you?"

Aaron nodded vigorously as she set out a cone for him. If only all of her problems would be so simple to fix.

* * *

On the way to Summer Shores Hospital, Kaleigh took a deep breath and prepped Aaron for what was about to happen.

"Mommy is going to follow around a doctor today to see what I might be doing for a job."

"Are you going to be a doctor?"

"No. More like a doctor's helper, if I can finish all the classes."

"You can finish. You're so smart!"

Kaleigh smiled for Aaron's sake and hoped her smarts would be enough to save them today.

She knew Aaron would behave himself, but for good measure, she reminded him, "You have to stay with me and be quiet, except to say hello and answer any questions you're asked. Okay?"

"Okay."

"Kids aren't allowed to work in the hospital, but let's see if they can make a special exception for us."

"What's an essesion?"

"An exception is when people treat us differently than the rules say to because we need extra help."

"I'll be really good."

"I know, honey."

Kaleigh took Aaron by the hand through the hospital parking lot and checked in with security.

The guard struck an intimidating figure—he was nearly as wide as he was tall—but he took the time to chat with Aaron. He printed out a badge for them both, and directed them to an elevator past the

13

hospital cafeteria.

After riding up to the top floor, Kaleigh checked in with the floor's receptionist. The woman eyed Aaron from behind a wide table. "Ms. Taylor, I thought you were a PTA applicant?" she asked.

"Yes, that's right."

"I'm afraid it's against hospital policy for trainees to take additional guests into patient rooms."

"I understand. I was wondering if I might please speak with Dr. Reynolds?" Recalling the doctor's kind face on her website photo, Kaleigh risked seeming impertinent.

Dr. Reynolds' "About Me" blurb had mentioned caring deeply for patients of all ages. Maybe she would be willing to hear Kaleigh out. If not, Kaleigh wasn't sure what her next step could be.

"She's in with a patient right now, but I'll get my colleague to check for you."

"Thank you."

They took their seats on the gray-blue waiting room chairs. Kaleigh tapped her nails on her seat's metal arm and tried to shake the sense that her world was falling apart. She didn't want to scare Aaron. She sat taller as the receptionist waved over another worker and whispered in her ear.

"It will be just a moment," the newcomer called to Kaleigh.

The nurse disappeared through the wing's double doors, only to return with who Kaleigh assumed was Dr. Reynolds.

The doctor's expression was friendly, albeit confused, as she pushed a pair of black spectacles over her barely-contained updo of pale, frizzy hair.

"Dr. Reynolds?" Kaleigh rose, and the doctor nodded. "I'm Kaleigh Taylor. I'd like to thank you for this opportunity. My babysitter…left town and I don't think she's coming back. I don't have any other childcare options. I wondered if I could take my son with me today?"

"I'm so sorry, but I'm afraid that's impossible. We'll have to reschedule."

"He won't make a sound."

She raised a skeptical eyebrow at that. "Even if we obtained a patient's consent, the liability would be significant."

"He won't touch anything either." In truth, the poor child was standing there like a statue, trying to give his mother a fighting chance.

"I don't mind if these two step in to my appointment." A familiar, irritating voice wafted over from the other end of the waiting room. "Really. It will take my mind off the exercises."

Kaleigh couldn't believe she hadn't recognized Jackson when she sat down a moment ago. In her defense, he had been facing away from them, wearing a backwards-facing baseball cap that covered his dark hair.

This guy is unbelievable, Kaleigh thought. *Always around when I embarrass myself.*

"You two know each other?" the doctor asked.

How should I respond? This is my latest mistake? My thorn-in-the-side coworker?

"Oh yeah, we're close friends," Jackson said and smiled broadly. Kaleigh wouldn't contradict him this time.

Dr. Reynolds tapped her lip, then sighed. "All right. Since he's in a private room, you two can sit in on Mr. Green's appointment and get one hour's credit for today. But you'll have to figure something else out for next time. Unfortunately, we don't offer a nursery service for volunteers. Maybe try one of those online nanny finders."

"Of course." Kaleigh nodded, grateful the doctor had granted her at least a little more time.

Dr. Reynolds turned to Jackson. "You're up next anyway." She scanned her key card at the doors. "You all can go to room four while I grab his chart."

Not meeting Jackson's eyes, Kaleigh steered Aaron down the hall and to the room's spare seat. Aaron happily accepted the muted game console she pulled from her bag (the product of her Christmas overtime). Then, Kaleigh retreated to the wall, eager to show that, despite her unorthodox demands, she was prepared to listen and learn.

Jackson sat on the treatment table, his massive legs dangling off the end.

Dr. Reynolds entered. "How have you been feeling?"

"Great."

"Have you been doing your exercises at home?"

15

"Every day."

"Let's see how your range of motion is progressing, then."

Kaleigh leaned forward as the doctor led Jackson through a series of leg stretches, occasionally instructing him to bend his knee a little more, or gently pressing his shoulder down to correct its position.

It was awkward watching her coworker basically conduct a workout session in her presence. She wasn't sure what prompted Jackson's need for physical therapy, but he seemed in perfect health to her.

Don't you dare ogle him, Kaleigh told herself. *You're at work.*

Kaleigh's favorite part of the strengthening exercises was when Dr. Reynolds gave Jackson a band between his knees and made him scuttle from wall to wall like a crab. She had to bite the inside of her mouth to keep from laughing.

After inspecting Jackson, Dr. Reynolds said, "All right, your knee is progressing well. You're clear to resume all normal activity. I'll send your release form to—"

"Great. Thanks, doc." Something akin to fear flickered beyond Jackson's eyes, and then it was gone. *Weird.*

"Thank you for letting our volunteer observe today." Dr. Reynolds turned to Kaleigh. "We'll talk more at our next session, when you have a sitter in place? Mrs. Clemons will take care of your paperwork."

Kaleigh nodded. "Thank you so much. Come on, Aaron." Aaron hopped off his chair and dutifully followed behind.

Jackson tailed them back to the reception desk. "Did you have a nice time?"

She bit back a retort about how thrilling it was to wonder if she was ever going to have the chance to see another session. Instead, she settled on a comment from lighter territory. "I did, and, may I say, it takes a very secure man to do yoga."

Jackson stretched his back and groaned. "Yeah. I've never been more flexible. I think I'll try goat yoga next."

"That I'd like to see."

"Name the time and place. I'm all yours."

"Ugh, forget I said anything."

Mrs. Clemons stamped Kaleigh's log sheet for the full hour, which was generous, considering that Jackson's appointment hadn't taken that long. Still, the column of remaining empty boxes stared up at her.

"How many hours do you have left?" Jackson asked, as if he heard her internal freak-out.

"Nine. But we are 'encouraged to do more' to get a competitive advantage." Kaleigh shook her head, thanked Mrs. Clemons, and headed for the elevator.

"You're trying to be a physical therapist?"

"A therapist's assistant." The elevator doors closed in front of them. The small space smelled of new paint, doubling the suffocating sensation of playing twenty questions with Jackson.

"You know," he fiddled with his wristwatch, "I could help you babysit."

"That's not an option."

He met her stare. "Why is that not an option?"

"I don't trust you." They stepped out of the elevator after it dinged on the ground floor.

Jackson gestured toward the cafeteria. "We can sit right here until you're done."

"You're going to come to the hospital once a week to hang out in a cafeteria with a little kid? Why?"

"I know you think I'm a horrible person. I hurt you the last time I tried to date you." He held a finger up, asking her to let him finish. "I shouldn't have talked to you and Ava at the same time. But I'm not trying to manipulate you into going out with me again. I've almost given up hope on that one. I do care about what happens to you, and I want you to get these hours. No one works harder than you. And if this is something that you want to do, for you and for your son, then I want to help you do it."

She couldn't believe him. Guys had lied to her all her life, and just because Jackson had found all the right words didn't mean he could be counted on. Yet, what other choice did she have?

Kaleigh glanced at the cafeteria workers, and then at the security guard, who had taken the extra time with Aaron today. Maybe if he worked here often, he would agree to keep an eye out for her son.

Kaleigh would make sure the officer knew the particulars of the unusual childcare agreement: one mother, leaving one child with one adult who was not allowed to take him off the premises. "I'll have to ask Aaron," she said finally.

"It's okay," Aaron chimed in. "You can go, Mommy. It will be boys only!" Evidently, he had followed their whole conversation.

Kaleigh sighed. Aaron's enthusiasm might make things harder. She would have to ensure that he knew the details of the situation as well.

"All right, Green. You start next week."

"I won't let you down, khaki pants," Jackson said, staring down at her uniform.

His toothsome grin matched his elementary sense of humor and laid a whole new layer of doubt on the whole "adult supervision" thing. As if he was beginning to sense her moods, he schooled his expression, gazed into her eyes, and said, "I promise."

3

The day of Kaleigh's second volunteering shift, Jackson noticed that her glance darted to him and Aaron as she briefed the security guard. It stung that she thought there was even a small chance that Jackson might leave, or snatch her kid.

The guard raised his arms in protest initially, but whatever Kaleigh said next must have convinced him. Jackson was learning that small-townspeople tended to be more accommodating than the people he grew up with in a bigger city. Kaleigh's smile was bright as she bounced back in their direction.

Jackson turned to Aaron. "Do you want something to eat?"

Aaron dropped his blue kids tablet on the beige laminate of the cafeteria table in his excitement to check out the menu, but then he paused to look back at his mother.

"Sure, I can get it," she said.

"Please, this is my treat. It's about time I start making up for all the headaches I give you."

She shrugged. "Can't argue with that."

"Can I get a chocolate muffin with apple juice?" Aaron asked, eyeballing the pictures above the serving area from afar.

"Sure thing, buddy." Jackson waved him over to go pick out the treat.

Kaleigh called out to him, "I'll be back as soon as I can." Pain lined her face.

"Okay, Mommy," Aaron hollered back, unconcerned.

Rising to join the boy in the lunch line, Jackson was glad that Aaron, at least, felt comfortable hanging out with him. "He'll be all right," Jackson said.

"He'd better be." Kaleigh jabbed a finger in his chest. Her navy work polo brought out the blue in her stormy eyes, and though they tempted him to linger longer, Jackson trotted over to Aaron in proof that he was committed to his new job.

From the line, he watched Kaleigh retreat to the elevator, a solitary figure with her shoulders taut. Posture strong.

Jackson felt alone often, but really, he was only a button-press away from a stack of takeout containers or a private car that could take him to the ice rink or wherever he wanted to go. Who could Kaleigh call when she needed something?

Prayers still felt foreign to his lips as a new church convert, but he couldn't help but think, *Please, God, let this school work out for her.* She was trying so hard.

Jackson just grabbed a vanilla snack cake for himself, since he'd drunk his morning protein shake already. He handed his debit card to the cashier, considering the many thousands of dollars that cushioned his bank account.

He wished Kaleigh would let him do more than buy her boy a baked good, but understood that her trust had to be earned. His botched breakup with Ava this summer hadn't helped him toward that goal.

"Thanks for the food, Jackson!" Aaron said.

"My pleasure, kid." Jackson ruffled the top of Aaron's sunny crop of hair. Jackson hadn't even taken his receipt before Aaron ran back to their table with his treasures, forcing Jackson to jog behind. As a babysitting novice, he wasn't letting Aaron out of his sight, even though Aaron seemed like a fun-sized adult compared to other tiny terrors he had come across while working at Hydrangea.

"So, what's your favorite game to play on your tablet?" Jackson asked.

"A racing game."

"Racing, huh? Is there two-player mode?"

"Yeah. Do you want to play with me?"

"Sure."

Aaron's mouth dropped open. "I didn't know grown-ups liked to play video games."

Jackson leaned close and whispered, "I guess I'm not really a grown-up." He twirled his packaged sponge cake on top of the table to emphasize the point.

Aaron giggled and scarfed down his muffin. Jackson helped Aaron clean his hands before powering up the tablet.

"I want to race with the red car," Aaron said.

"You got it."

The hour passed quickly thanks to Aaron's enthusiasm. In no time, Kaleigh appeared at Jackson's side, causing him to startle and lift his finger from the touchscreen. This sent his race car careening into a pool of water.

His loss prompted yet another victory dance from Aaron—Jackson's opponent's small fingers had been unexpectedly nimble on the device.

"Mommy, I won way more games than Jackson!" Aaron said.

"The kid's had time to practice," Jackson muttered.

Kaleigh's smile fell. "I do limit his screen time at home."

Jackson couldn't believe he'd said the wrong thing again. He had meant it as a joke.

Aaron, however, wasn't fazed. He stuck his tongue out in disgust. "Mom is always turning off my tablet and taking me to the library."

Kaleigh packed up Aaron's tablet and juice bottle. "You'll thank me for it one day." She patted the top of his head. "All right, I guess you can kick Jackson's butt another day. It's time to go home."

"Aww!"

"We'll come back next week." She raised an eyebrow. "If Jackson's able to make it?"

Jackson met her gaze. "I'll be here."

* * *

"I'll be there."

As cute as Aaron's grin was as he showed Kaleigh his mastery of colors and numbers, correctly matching balls of modeling clay to the corresponding sheets of paper she'd prepared for him, Jackson's declaration kept tugging at her mind.

Not only had Jackson been there for his first babysitting appointment, he'd arrived before Kaleigh. He'd shown Aaron the time of his life and then didn't retaliate when Kaleigh gave him a hard time about the screen time comment.

In retrospect, she could see how pointing out Aaron's video games skills wasn't a dig at her parenting. But any hint of questioning about how she was doing at that job poked the tender doubts that she constantly carried.

Every day it seemed, new articles populated on her news and social media feeds about what was good for children. She wanted to do what was best for Aaron, of course, but the quantity and dramatic headlines of the articles left her feeling overwhelmed.

She didn't have unlimited resources to always give him the academic edge, keep up with the healthiest recipes, or reap the benefits of the latest psychological theories.

Kaleigh didn't have anyone to talk with about the decisions she made, including her newest and most important decision of all: once Aaron went to bed and she could focus, Kaleigh would need to follow up on Dr. Reynold's advice and search for a new caregiver online.

Jackson had helped her with her volunteering dilemma, but now Kaleigh needed to find someone reliable to take over for Lana while she kept and even increased her scheduled shifts at Hydrangea. It would be a miracle to find any sitter who was affordable enough.

Just thinking about the choice created a tight, throbbing band around Kaleigh's forehead, but she needed to push her worries aside. She would search for childcare later tonight, exhausted or not. There was no use stressing before then.

* * *

Jackson lounged on his living room sofa, trying to pass the evening by playing his favorite World War II video game, but he just kept losing.

He dropped the controller and sighed, deciding to face what was really on his mind. It took exactly three thumb strokes on his phone screen for Jackson to pull up the familiar email. "Please Complete in the Next Six Months for Your January Term of Service," its subject line read.

He re-scanned the body of the message. "To-do Before Volunteering in Costa Rica: Obtain medical clearance"—done. "Go shopping according to the attached checklist"—done.

The minute Jackson received the onboarding notice back in June, he'd asked D'Angelo to take him to a sporting goods store. There, he picked up professional-grade neon balls and collapsible soccer nets. With less enthusiasm, Jackson purchased the recommended flashlight and head lamp. These items made him wonder how good his access to power would be.

The ultra-cushy sleeping bag he found was going to be a major downgrade from his king-sized, memory foam mattress. There was also the difficulty that no travel-sized portions of his favorite hair gel existed to take with him on the plane.

Yes, the journey would be an adjustment, but it would be worth it. After years of dreaming about packing up and leaving, out of reach of his parents' disapproval, this was happening.

Guilt surged in his stomach as a text came through from Kaleigh, confirming the time for next week's babysitting session. *What will she do about Aaron when I leave?*

Jackson shoved that thought down. He had months to figure out how to tell her that he had plans to fly to another country. Five months, to be exact.

Jackson had talked to D'Angleo about caring for Duke through the next year, and had notified Miss Lewis about his upcoming departure.

He wished, once his parents found out about the trip and cut him off, he would still have enough money to keep both of them in his employ, but he wasn't sure he would. If he didn't, Jackson wanted to make sure Miss Lewis had plenty of time to line up another position.

He'd even been teaching himself to speak Spanish using an app on his phone. It was amazing how Jackson's characteristic aversion to studying had melted away with the proper motivation. His dad would accuse him of being lazy, of not prioritizing a real job, but Jackson knew he would finally be doing something important. He felt ready to leave in days, not months.

He ran his hand absentmindedly over the arm of his black leather sofa. He felt ready, apart from one red-haired problem left to solve.

4

Mrs. McCauley lived in the Taylors' apartment complex and had two dozen five-star reviews on SitterBug.com, but the woman was still a complete stranger. Everyone reviewing her was a complete stranger. How could Kaleigh leave her child with a stranger?

Walking across the complex to interview the *stranger* taking charge of Aaron felt like all too much. In a fit of rage, Kaleigh punched the wall of Building Three. *Ow. That was stupid.*

Throbbing knuckles couldn't distract Kaleigh from the fury which consumed her at the thought that her own mother had put them in this situation. Lana must have assumed that her moaned complaints would be enough of a warning, but she'd been complaining for Kaleigh's entire life. Kaleigh hadn't expected Lana to abandon them.

Mrs. McCauley's door sported a wreath of bright gold, orange, and red leaves. Kaleigh pressed the doorbell before she could decide to turn back.

When the door creaked open, it felt strange to have been so afraid of this hunched-over woman who was even shorter than Kaleigh. Her white hair was cut close to her scalp. Her smile shone with pink gloss that matched her knobby cardigan, and her home smelled of rose oil and vanilla. Still, this was the woman Kaleigh was going to trust with the most precious person in her world.

As if sensing her nervousness, Mrs. McCauley reached out a wizened hand to gently touch Kaleigh's elbow. "You must be Kaleigh.

Come in, dear." She shuffled to a maroon sofa and tapped the worn-out cushion next to her.

Kaleigh sunk down in the cushy seat. "Thank you for agreeing to meet in-person. I know you're a certified sitter, with lots of experience."

Mrs. McCauley waved away that title. "Of course you wanted to meet with me. You can only tell so much from a computer screen." She turned to face a small bookshelf beside her seat, littered with dozens of framed photos. "These are my babies. My natural ones," she pointed to a picture of a trio of adults, linked arm and arm, "and all the ones I've cared for over the years. I thought it was time to give it up, but the truth is, I missed the company. I didn't last a year into retirement. My daughter got me set up on that babysitting website thingy." Her brow crinkled when she mentioned technology, but smoothed out again as she gazed over her collection of treasures.

Next to the pictures were scribbles on faded coloring book pages and handprint Christmas ornaments, though winter was still months away. The top shelf held gossip magazines, the television remote, and a single cup of coffee with the word "Mom" in a heart printed on it in easy reach.

"I can't pay you much," Kaleigh blurted out. "I can do thirty dollars a shift." It would still be tight, though only half as much as what the other nannies on the website were charging.

"That's all right, you just give me what you can. Now, what would you say to some chocolate-chip cookies?"

Kaleigh's mouth, once poised to deliver a brilliant defense, snapped shut. She wanted to cry. Mrs. McCauley seemed like the grandmother, or mother, for that matter, that she always dreamed about—generous and peaceful.

Kaleigh was glad when the older lady started bustling around the kitchen so she could collect herself. It was as if Mrs. McCauley knew that Aaron wasn't the only one who needed looking after.

Like a dam worn down by the weight of time, each new wave of kindness put another fissure in her heart, trying to break through the mistrust and skepticism that had kept her safe since childhood. Now, she was feeling less like an impenetrable dam and more like a little sailboat, subject to the will of the wind as she relied on first Jackson and now Mrs. McCauley.

Lana had destroyed all the stability Kaleigh thought she'd had. Hopefully, for Aaron's sake, they could both stay afloat.

* * *

Kaleigh noticed that Jackson stood across from her in the circle of employees at Hydrangea's morning meeting. She was used to ignoring him at work, but it didn't seem right now that they had a standing childcare arrangement.

She gave him a brisk nod, which caused a grin to break across his face. *I wonder what smart remark he's making in his head right now,* Kaleigh thought. He raised one dark eyebrow above his light green eyes, and the bold expression spiked Kaleigh's blood as if Jackson had started a grade-school staring contest.

Their manager cleared her throat, distracting Kaleigh from getting too lost in Jackson's smoulder. Kaleigh shook herself, feeling physically tainted. She really had to stop giving the man so much attention.

The boss was rocking a magenta jumpsuit with a black blazer and strappy heels, but Kaleigh was grateful Jenny allowed the employees to wear a more comfortable, business-casual look at work. Flats and khakis were just fine with Kaleigh.

Despite her tortuous footwear, Jenny stood with ramrod-straight posture as she addressed the circle. "This morning, you all get to be a part of something special. At 9:30, we are hosting a private birthday party for a girl named Nora, so we won't be opening at our normal time. I need most of you to clean the store. Would anyone like to prep the charm bracelets instead?"

Cleaning? Eww. Kaleigh's hand shot up at the same time as Jackson's. *Oops.*

"Thank you. Each child at the party gets to make a bracelet for free, so we'll need to have plenty of cords and beads ready to go."

"You got it, boss." Jackson saluted.

"Let's get started." Jenny sent the employees off with a single clap.

Though she was awkwardly paired off with Jackson, Kaleigh looked forward to the change of pace from her normal schedule. The two walked back to the stockroom where the bracelet materials were arranged in clear boxes, stacked on metal shelves above a small white table. Jackson sat at the table first. Kaleigh took the folding chair by Jackson's side, but casually scooted it as far away as possible until she was almost against the wall.

She grabbed a spool of elastic cord and began to unwind, measure, cut, and stretch out strings for the bracelets. Jackson took down their most popular beads and charms to arrange in more child-friendly organizers, with different cubbies that the girls could grab from. He emptied out bubble-gum pink, clear purple, faux-crystal, and unicorn pieces into the wide, square compartments.

At the picture of Jackson surrounded by so much sparkle, Kaleigh asked, "How'd you end up working in a girl's clothing store?"

"My dad is an area manager back home in Iowa. He's overseen eight successful stores. Now, he's up for regional manager, on track to be a VP for Hydrangea."

"Impressive," she said, trying to listen while not losing count of how many cords she had cut so far.

"Yeah, it's great," Jackson said, chagrined. "And my mom's a broadcast journalist for our local news station. Then you have me, the failure."

Kaleigh raised her eyebrows.

"I got my business degree like I was supposed to, and have since shown zero interest in doing anything with it. To be honest, right now my dad thinks I'm a coordinator at this store and not a sales associate."

"Well, with your killer work ethic, I can't believe Jenny hasn't promoted you already," Kaleigh remarked wryly. They both knew that, while Jackson's attendance record was better than hers, during his shifts, he put in the bare minimum required to stay employed.

"I wouldn't take the promotion, even if Jenny offered it. I don't want to be my father. For once, I want to be happy with where I'm at, and choosing the kind of life he's lived would be doing the exact opposite. At least while I'm working so far away, some of the heat is off my back."

"I never heard of anyone moving to Florida to escape the heat," Kaleigh quipped.

Jackson paused. "Kaleigh Taylor. Was that a joke I just heard?"

She flipped her braid over her shoulder. "Don't get used to it." Maybe she was joking around too much. It was unlike her, but Jackson seemed so sad.

"Anyway. The problem is, I like living at a certain standard, and my father has threatened to cut me off if I 'waste' any more of his money." Jackson rolled up the sleeves of his mint green button-down, and for a moment, Kaleigh was distracted by the contrast of the light color with the tanned skin of his forearm. She could imagine how a month's worth of workout supplements and professional dry cleaning could set a person back.

Jackson continued, "He doesn't know that I've opened my own bank account, and I'm saving up enough to make it on my own."

Kaleigh couldn't relate to Jackson's "rich dad, poor me" line of thinking, but the desire for independence, she understood completely.

"Can I ask about your family?" Jackson asked.

Kaleigh stiffened. "You can ask, but I may not answer."

He nodded. "I'm mainly wondering, do you have anyone at home to help you? I mean, it seems like you have to call out a lot."

"I used to have someone at home," she said, attempting to sound casual. "But my mother had other places to be."

"Who's watching Aaron now?"

"A neighbor lady I found on one of those caregiver search sites. She came with great recommendations, but it's still really hard to leave him behind."

"Isn't he old enough to go to school?"

"He's turning five in a month, so he'll start kindergarten next year." She shook her head. "And that's another problem. The school we're zoned for isn't great, but we can't afford private school."

"I know a teacher. I'll ask him what he thinks."

"It couldn't hurt." She paused. "You're not trying to get out of babysitting at the hospital, are you?"

Though Kaleigh had kept her eyes glued down at her work, she could hear Jackson exhale as if he was frustrated with her again. But then, he shocked her by resting a hand on her shoulder. She lifted her head.

"I don't mind babysitting," he said slowly, as if he really wanted her to hear him. "Aaron's great. And I'm glad I can take a small part of the burden off your shoulders."

Kaleigh's mouth opened, but she couldn't quite think of any words to say. Suddenly, the stockroom door swung open, and Kaleigh nearly jumped out of her skin. She managed to scoot her chair another two inches away from Jackson's.

Mariana took a feather duster from its hook on the wall. "Hi, guys," she said, looking from one sheepish expression to the next. She seemed to shrug off her confusion to ask, "Jackson, did you rent the cotton candy machine yet?"

"I'm all set to pick it up next Friday afternoon."

"Perfect! I'll see you tonight, then." She left, and Kaleigh felt like someone dropped a bar of lead into her stomach. *I should have known.*

"I thought Mariana had a boyfriend," Kaleigh said lightly.

"She does," Jackson said, not understanding her implication. After an awkward pause, he caught on. "I'll see them both at Bible study tonight."

"You go to Bible study?"

He slapped a hand to his heart. "Ouch, don't sound so surprised."

She shook her head. "No, I don't mean that in a bad way. I just mean... you and Mariana don't seem like the type to hit people over the head with a Bible."

"Maybe when I get one, I'll give it a try." Jackson smiled, swatting her with an imaginary rectangle. She ducked, playing along, but also unnerved by the thought of him touching her again. "I have been reading the Gospels on my phone," he said.

Kaleigh changed the subject. If Jackson was trying to evangelize to her, he was wasting his time. "What's the deal with the cotton candy machine?"

He waved his hand across the air as if showing her a banner. "Cotton Candy for Cans. It's our booth's theme for the town's fall festival."

"That's nice. Are you collecting for that local food pantry?"

"Yep. You and Aaron should come by."

"It's a little early for a fall fest. It's still ninety degrees outside."

"I know. But you Floridians seem so eager to start your pretend autumn season. Please tell me it actually gets cold here at some point."

Kaleigh shrugged. "Not until November at least."

"I guess I can understand why they don't want to hold off the celebrating then. You should at least think about coming. They'll have pumpkins, a bounce house, a corn maze..."

"I told you not to ask me out anymore."

Jackson's expression was innocent. "I didn't ask you out. I'm just saying that we may happen to be at a town function at the same time. Ten a.m. to be exact. At the booth by the playground."

"Playground?" This event was sounding like something Aaron would like. "What day is it?"

"Saturday, September 6th. You're not working until the evening that day—I already checked the schedule Jenny posted."

"Did you now?" Kaleigh rolled her eyes. "We'll see."

But she could tell, to Jackson's over-eager brain, all he heard was a "yes."

5

Jackson came into the fellowship hall Wednesday night and headed straight for the chair next to Pete. Pete's eyebrows raised at this rare, voluntary contact, but he still offered Jackson a polite, "Hey, how's it going?" as if they hadn't been avoiding each other for the past month.

"I'm fine." Jackson was only a few minutes early to Bible study, so he needed to get straight to the point. "The school where you teach, is it a good one?"

Pete adjusted his glasses. "It's the best in the county. Why?"

"I have a friend whose son really needs somewhere to go for kindergarten next year. Would it be free?"

"Yeah. We get federal funding for our students. We have a long waiting list, but as a faculty member, I may have a little pull."

"I promise, there would be no one more deserving than these two."

"In that case, let me see if I can get your friend an application."

Jackson shook Pete's hand vigorously. "Thank you. I really appreciate this. I think the mom might be coming to the Fall Festival, so maybe she can chat with you there."

"Sure thing."

Ava stuck an eager head around her boyfriend's shoulder. "Would this 'mom' be Kaleigh?"

To Ava's left, Jess Wilson also poked her head in Jackson's direction. "Who's Kaleigh?"

31

Jackson looked down at his smart watch. "Wow, is it seven already?" he called out, loud enough for Pastor Thomas to hear.

The older man startled and cleared his throat. "Let's begin in Romans chapter eleven."

Jackson pulled the chapter up on his phone, and the pastor asked, "Jackson, would you please read verses fifteen and sixteen aloud?"

Jackson cleared his throat. He didn't get nervous over much, but reading scripture in front of even a handful of church members was way outside of his comfort zone.

He shifted in his chair and brought the screen close to his face, steadying his shaking elbows on the plastic table in front of him. "For he saith to Moses, I will have mercy on whom I will have mercy, and I will have compassion on whom I will have compassion. So then it is not of him that willeth, nor of him that runneth, but of God that sheweth mercy."

"Thank you." Pastor Thomas nodded in his direction, and Jackson exhaled. He had jumped off cliffs and parasailed over the ocean, but being called out in this crowd sure could make him sweat. He skimmed over the words again, since, in the moment before, he had been more focused on speaking than on listening.

"Have any of you ever felt like you were running through life? Like you wanted something so bad, you'd climb any mountain or enter any race to get there?" A few people raised their hands. "I think most of us relate to that feeling. But God doesn't think like us, does He?"

Across the table, a man whose name Jackson hadn't learned yet curved his lips into a knowing smirk. Jackson wasn't in on the joke, however. In his mind, he echoed Pastor Thomas's question: *Does He?*

"Sometimes we can wish and work so hard that we think God is going to look down and grant us anything we want. The truth is that what we really need to be is still, and trusting that He already knows what He's doing."

Pastor Thomas's words ran contrary to everything Jackson had been taught. His dad had taught him that, without ambition, he was nothing, so he should work as hard as he could to get money and respect.

"God knew what He was doing when He called each of you to be here tonight. He has been compassionate to us, the undeserving. So how can we think less of ourselves—of our abilities, even of our failures—and start leaning more on Him?"

Isaac Wilson piped up, "We can do good for others, even when it doesn't benefit us."

*When it doesn't benefit us...*Jackson felt like he was so far away from what this book taught. He'd tried to take Isaac's advice to talk to Kaleigh softly, but now he had to step it up and question his own motivations.

Kaleigh kept accusing him of trying to get something from their relationship, of not being truly committed. The accusations grated when, for the first time in his life, he was only trying to do right by someone. But would he really be okay if, at the end of her volunteer hours, she didn't want to spend time with him again?

Pastor Thomas had called the circle of people gathered there "the undeserving." As Jackson looked around the room at teachers, nurses, and loving parents, he knew that "undeserving" was not the label he would choose to attach to any of the members.

But if Pastor Thomas lumped them all together as being unable to earn God's love by their own strength, maybe Jackson wasn't as left out as he felt. Maybe, by God's mercy, there could be a way for him to change, to become like them and the other Christians he'd been reading about.

The heroes in the Bible didn't seem to be the traditional, swaggering, red-cape types. He racked his brain for the name—*John the Baptist*—even ran around in camel hair and leather. Yet Jesus called him the greatest prophet of all?

Jackson sure had a lot to learn about God's way of thinking. If only he could learn enough to be strong and steady for Kaleigh. He hoped to continue making strides, starting next Wednesday at the hospital.

* * *

The morning of her third volunteer shift, Kaleigh found it easier to leave Aaron with Jackson in the hospital cafeteria. Last time, Aaron raved about their time together. Her nerves today had more to do with her own performance.

During the previous week's observation, Kaleigh had followed Dr. Reynolds to two patient sessions. She'd tried to take notes, but, honestly, she didn't know what she was supposed to be taking note of. Despite taking a basic anatomy class in high school, she hadn't learned enough about the muscles the therapist was working on to be able to know what she was watching.

She only nodded as Dr. Reynolds spat out the names of the different exercises, and shook her head when the doctor asked if she had any questions. It was so over her head, she didn't know what questions to ask.

Mrs. Clemons, who Kaleigh learned was called a "Medical Support Assistant," directed Kaleigh to the office that Dr. Reynolds shared with a few other therapists. The office smelled of freshly brewed coffee.

Dr. Reynolds wore baby pink scrubs today and was peering at x-rays on a screen when Kaleigh arrived. She looked up and smiled. "Hi, there."

"Hi."

"Have a seat." She gestured to a vacant chair beside her, and typed one last notation on the computer before closing out the image.

"I wanted to touch base with you about our last visit. Did you learn a lot?"

Kaleigh swallowed. "Mm-hm."

Dr. Reynolds threw her head back. Her laugh tinkled like fairy bells. "That's what I thought." She scooted her desk chair closer to Kaleigh's and rested her elbows on her knees. "I remember what it was like to be a student observer, back when dinosaurs roamed the earth."

Kaleigh snorted. The doctor looked no older than forty, but she appreciated the attempt to make her feel comfortable.

Dr. Reynolds continued, "It can be overwhelming. I thought you might want some advice today, now that my schedule's not so slammed."

The tension left Kaleigh's shoulders. "That would be great."

"Learning how to diagnose and treat the patient is critical, of course, but it's just as important to learn how to approach the patient."

"Oh." The doctor was talking about people skills, which were not exactly Kaleigh's strong suit. Apparently, Dr. Reynold's shrewd eyes hadn't missed Kaleigh's reluctance to approach the patients. "I didn't want to overstep," Kaleigh hedged.

"Well, today, overstep."

Awesome, Kaleigh thought—evidence that sarcasm came to her as naturally as blinking. This was going to be a challenge.

Kaleigh's main positive interactions these days included conversations about horseys and construction vehicles. There was nothing tough about being approachable to a kid. In conversations with adults, however, she preferred a less-is-more approach.

That'd certainly been safer whenever she talked with Lana. And last week at Hydrangea, when Kaleigh had basically spilled her life story to Jackson, the slip had made her feel unnervingly out-of-control.

But, if Kaleigh needed to open up more to be a Therapist's Assistant, then that's what she was going to do.

Mrs. Clemons popped her head in the doorway. "Mr. Meyer is ready for you."

"Thanks, Jeanie." Dr. Reynolds stood, and Kaleigh followed suit. "Our first appointment today is with Richard Meyer. We've been working to decrease the pain in his shoulder." She plucked up her aqua clipboard and led Kaleigh to room three near the end of the hall.

After a brief knock, Dr. Reynolds opened the door to reveal an older man, slouched on the examination table. His hair shined dark silver, and his brown eyes brimmed with antagonism. Kaleigh held back another snort. *I'm supposed to act all warm and fuzzy with this guy?*

She constructed what she hoped was a friendly smile, but his gaze was fixed on the doctor. He crossed his arms. "I'm here," he said. "Let's get this over with."

Glancing over her notes, Dr. Reynold's voice was chipper. "Okay, it looks like we're due for some shoulder strengthening. I'll be right back with a dowel rod." She pivoted back toward the door. "Kaleigh, why don't you keep Mr. Meyer company for a moment, and I'll be right back."

Kaleigh wondered if Dr. Reynolds had truly forgotten the dowel rod, or if she'd just carefully constructed a trial-by-fire. She hoped her panic didn't show on her face.

"So," Kaleigh started, "what brings you here?"

"My son's nagging," he spat.

Okay, let's try a different approach, Kaleigh thought. "What do you like to do in your spare time?" *People enjoy talking about their interests, right?*

Wrong.

Mr. Meyer leaned close, as if revealing a secret. "I like to come to the hospital, aggravate my aching shoulder, and talk with a nosy teenage girl." He yanked his phone out of his plaid shirt pocket to check the time.

Kaleigh balled up her hands on her hips. "I'm twenty-two." *And too tough to be discouraged by the likes of you.*

With a deep breath, Kaleigh reminded herself to be gentle. After all, people often accused her of being heartless, when she was simply slow to trust.

Kaleigh caught a glimpse of the logo on Mr. Meyer's phone case, glad that Lana's second boyfriend had been obsessed with baseball. It took her a second to recall the team name.

"You're a Mariners fan, huh?"

"Yeah," he groused.

"Do you want me to put a game on TV while you wait?"

The cantankerous man didn't answer directly, but a casual shrug of his shoulders told her she'd hit her mark.

After she found the correct channel, Kaleigh didn't fill the room with any more chatter. Instead, she sat down in one of the guest chairs and watched the game with him until Dr. Reynolds reappeared, rod in hand.

Kaleigh hopped to her feet and took notes as Dr. Reynolds guided Mr. Meyer through a series of exercises. She knew she wasn't writing down the correct terminology, but tried to at least record a summary of the therapist's different techniques.

Most of the time, Mr. Meyer was able to keep his attention on the TV, but one stretch seemed to be more difficult for him.

The doctor placed her fingers lightly on the top of the dowel rod, as he wasn't pushing at the correct angle with his left hand. The increased rotation caused his right shoulder to tremble, and tiny beads of sweat glistened on his temples. Dr. Reynolds relieved him after a few seconds.

"Go ahead and rest. Did Brandon install your pulley?"

Mr. Meyer grumbled, "He did, all right. And he's been on me to use it, too."

"Good." Dr. Reynolds smiled.

Kaleigh figured, based on Mr. Meyer's previous complaint, that Brandon was his son. She was impressed that, despite seeing dozens of patients every day, Dr. Reynolds was able to remember his name.

"All right," Dr. Reynolds said. "Great job. I'll see you next week."

Mr. Meyer grunted, but he gave Kaleigh a brisk nod before they left the room. Dr. Reynolds' eyebrows lifted.

Once they were far enough down the hallway, she said, "Well done."

Kaleigh mumbled, "I didn't do much," but her insides lifted with the praise.

She was glad, now, that Dr. Reynolds had stepped out and forced her to be on her own.

Kaleigh'd begun the PTA path because it seemed the most logical option. She liked athletics, needed decent benefits, and couldn't spend forever in college.

But, for the first time, Kaleigh envisioned herself working with the patients, enjoying the job instead of simply showing up for the paycheck. She could find out what they needed, even if it was just a smile on their face. She found that she looked forward to meeting Dr. Reynolds' next patient.

6

Jackson had assumed that Aaron would share his fortitude in playing video games hours on end. He'd thought that Aaron would love nothing better than to race digital cars with him for the duration of their second hangout. But, apparently, the kid was ready for something new.

"I'm bored," Aaron whined, dropping his tablet down on the table.

"Oh," Jackson powered the device off, at a loss of what else to suggest. "Well, what would you like to do?"

"Go outside!"

"Umm..." Jackson looked past the security checkpoint—a different guard was there than last week's—and out the automatic doors. "I'm not sure your mom would be good with that."

"Yeah, she would. Kids need fresh air."

Jackson peered through the hospital windows and spotted a circular walkway with a grassy area inside. A few workers ate their lunches at wrought-iron tables which surrounded the path and overlooked the street. It looked safe enough.

"Okay. As long as you promise to stick to the walkway. It shouldn't hurt to stretch our legs." Jackson picked up Aaron's tablet and they cleared away the leftover garbage from their snack. "Uh..." Jackson wasn't sure what the protocol was for escorting a four-year-old. "Does your mom hold your hand when you go outside?"

"Not on the sidewalk," he chirped. Still, Jackson quickened his pace as Aaron skipped out the doors. As athletic as he considered himself to be, Jackson soon broke into a sweat staying close to his charge.

After a few loops around the sidewalk, Aaron planted himself in the center of the grass, fell to his back, and started rolling back and forth. Jackson smirked. *A little weird, but I guess that's okay.*

Then, Aaron halted and let out a bloodcurdling scream. "Get them off me! Get them off me!" He thrashed on the ground, swiping his hands over his arms.

After a moment, Jackson spied the problem—an anthill crawling with fire ants. He unfroze from his stupor and yanked Aaron away from the small pile of sand.

"I still feel them," Aaron cried, so Jackson pulled off Aaron's t-shirt and shook it back and forth, flipping it inside out to dump out any insects still clinging to the seams.

Aaron quieted, still sniffling. After a careful inspection, Jackson helped him put his shirt back on.

Kaleigh's voice cut through the air behind them. "What do you think you're doing?" Her tone was murderous.

Jackson whirled around. "There were ants..."

"I mean, why are you outside? I never said you could take him outside."

"But Aaron asked me to."

Kaleigh skidded to a stop and put her arm around Aaron's shoulders. She lowered her tone. "He is a child. You are the adult. *You* are supposed to be in charge."

"I'm sorry, I didn't think you would mind."

"You didn't think I would mind?" Jackson saw tears glisten in Kaleigh's blue eyes before she furiously wiped them away with the back of her hand. "I didn't know where you were. I just happened to see you out the window." She grabbed Aaron's hand. "It's time to go."

His crying started up again, so Kaleigh lifted him in her arms and walked away.

Jackson's head was reeling. How did this happen? He had been so concerned with showing Aaron a good time that he proved himself to be a reckless babysitter. Numbly, he texted D'Angelo that his visit was over. *And it is probably over for good.*

* * *

Jackson forced himself to church that night, though he'd been tempted to stay home and mope around his apartment. However, Bible study hadn't distracted him from the sour memories of Kaleigh's livid expression or Aaron's fat tears.

"What'd you say?" Jackson asked, when he realized that Isaac had called his name a second time. They meandered out the church doors. The lowering sun cut the temperature nicely, and cicadas sang somewhere in the faraway trees.

"Are you thinking about that girl again?" Isaac asked.

"Yeah, sorry. I've got a lot on my mind."

"It might help to talk about it." Isaac gestured towards the pair of tan Adirondack chairs which faced the parking lot.

"You don't have to go home?" Jackson glanced back at the doors as Isaac's family exited. Noah was trying to wriggle out of his mother's arms.

"Come here, buddy." Isaac scooped up his son. "We drove separate tonight. Let me just get this guy to the car."

Jackson nodded and sank down in one of the chairs, watching glumly as Isaac carried Noah to his seat. On second thought, maybe Jackson wasn't in the mood to talk to Father-of-the-Year.

Isaac bounded back to sit by him. "Now. What's happening."

"I screwed up again." Jackson brushed a fly off his chair's arm, as if this major failure, too, was only a minor annoyance.

"Hmm," Isaac said. His silence implied that he was waiting for the rest of the story.

Jackson grimaced. "I took Aaron outside without asking first. It's not like I could've bothered Kaleigh with a bunch of questions while she was working. But we weren't there when she came back downstairs. She flipped out."

Isaac shook his head. "That sounds rough. It was an honest mistake, though."

Jackson threw his arms in the air. "Kaleigh's been waiting around for me to make a mistake. Now that I've proved her right, she'll never let me come back."

"Maybe if you tried explaining things to her..."

"What's the point? It took this long to get her to talk to me, and that was before I endangered the most important person in her life."

"But you did get her to talk to you. Are you ready to give up so quickly?"

Jackson shrugged. "I'm not the greatest at keeping long-term relationships."

"Well, you don't have to stay like that forever. With time, you can get better. Remember what Pastor Thomas says. God majors in impossible cases. You just have to decide if you're willing to put the work in. Kaleigh, is she worth struggling for?"

Jackson stared at the concrete beneath his feet. "She's the best girl I've ever known." He muttered, "Even if she is infuriating."

Isaac barked out a laugh. "That's usually how it goes." Suddenly, he leaned forward, looking out toward his black pickup truck. It was the only car left in the lot. "How did you get here?" he asked.

"My...driver dropped me off."

Isaac sat back and, after a moment, nodded politely. This was a kinder response than the open jealousy that Jackson was used to. Still, even if Jackson was an entitled brat who got chauffeured around, he didn't want Isaac to see him that way.

He blurted out, "I got in a car accident last June. It was my fault. I ran a red light, t-boned a girl and put myself in the hospital. I haven't driven since."

"Is that how you hurt your leg? I thought you said it was an old injury."

"Technically, it is. I did tear my meniscus once before, playing hockey. The accident tore it worse. I'm sorry, I didn't feel like getting into the details at the time. I wasn't proud of what I did." He hung his head. "I'm still not."

Isaac whistled. "Hey, no worries about not telling me. It sounds like you've got a couple tough things to face down."

"I think I'll start with Kaleigh. At least she's shot me down before. I should be used to it by now. I hope she doesn't rake me over the coals too bad about Aaron, though. I really do like the kid, and I never wanted to hurt him."

"Of course you didn't. Your intentions were good. Just try and be patient with her. Take it from a parent—reason goes out the window when your kid is involved."

Jackson nodded. "I should text my ride now."

"I can give you a ride."

"Are you sure?"

"Anytime."

"All right." Jackson texted D'Angelo the change in plans, and they walked to Isaac's truck.

"I have something to give you, anyway. Sorry I forgot to bring it to church." Isaac laughed. "Now I've got to remember Noah's shoes, his blanket, his cars, so anything extra I'm liable to leave behind."

When Jackson opened the passenger door, he saw a Bible on his seat. It had his name engraved on it in silver letters. As he stroked the indentations with his thumb, a lump formed in his throat that he quickly cleared away. "Thank you."

It was the most thoughtful gift he had ever received. Now he'd feel more like part of the group.

"No problem. We're glad to have you visiting, and everyone should have their own Bible. Maybe now you don't have to read off your phone."

Jackson slid in the truck and placed the Bible on his lap.

Isaac continued, "I highlighted a model prayer, given by Jesus in the book of Matthew. Prayer's a good discipline to start, too, if you're new to the faith. Chapter six outlines how to praise God, how to seek His will..."

"His will?"

"What the Lord would have you to do with your life. Sometimes we have one plan that we've been working toward, when really, God has something better in mind that we need to open our eyes to."

Jackson almost confided in Isaac then about going to Costa Rica, but he wasn't sure how he would react if Isaac cast doubt on that dream. An outside observer couldn't understand Jackson's need to flee the corporate life.

Jackson had to make his own mark on the world, in the opposite direction that his father had been pushing him toward since childhood. Costa Rica had kept him going for the longest time. If Jackson didn't go on his term of service, who would he be then?

Jackson may not have been ready to hear Isaac's advice on his travel plans, but he did need a wingman for his relationship problems.

"Do you mind if I text Kaleigh now?" he asked.

"Not at all." Isaac turned his music down so Jackson could concentrate, and pulled out of the parking lot.

Jackson: I'm sorry that I took Aaron out without permission. I made a bad call, and it won't happen again. I understand if you don't want me to babysit any more, but I'm happy to keep coming by, if you agree. Please don't let me be the reason you can't finish your observation hours.

Jackson's stomach clenched as he saw the three blinking dots that showed Kaleigh was typing. He thought, *At least she's responding*. After a few minutes, Kaleigh's reply appeared.

Kaleigh: Maybe I overreacted. I have to keep a tight watch on Aaron. I'm all he has.

Jackson: I understand.

Kaleigh: Make sure that you ask next time if you have a question about ANYTHING.

Jackson: I promise. Thank you. I'll see you Saturday at the festival, if you and Aaron are still able to make it.

He kept the reply short and straightforward, not wanting to push his luck now that they had come to a truce. He would try his best never to need one again.

7

Kaleigh and Aaron passed an ice cream truck on their way into the "fall" festival. This morning, Kaleigh'd anticipated the sweltering temperatures and wisely dressed in a light pink ribbed tank tucked into high-waisted shorts. The thermometer in her car had not yet hit ninety, but the bright sun always did its work in time.

Her sneakers kicked up little clouds of dust as they traversed the patchy grass. Aaron pulled her hand farther forward as the first few booths came into view.

Someone had hand-painted a sign proclaiming "Summer Shores Fall Festival" in cheery red script and hung it beside the hosting farm's barn. Next to the sign, the farmers had stacked bales of hay and pumpkins around an antique red tractor. Aaron sprinted up the giant wheels in record time and gave his best cheesy smile so that Kaleigh could snap a pic.

After he broke his pose, Aaron looked toward the farm's functioning tractor, where some teenagers were padding a trailer with more hay bales and blankets. "Mommy, can we do a hayride later?" he asked.

"Sure, but let's find Jackson first." Kaleigh's heart beat faster at the sound of his name. She shushed it and told herself that it was irrational that she should feel embarrassed of her behavior on Wednesday. Jackson had said he was sorry, and he was the one who put Aaron at risk.

Kaleigh had considered avoiding this trip altogether, but Aaron had been so excited to come to the festival that she couldn't refuse him.

Jackson came into view, and this time, Kaleigh's racing heart had nothing to do with anxiety. He was manning the money under the shade of his church's white tent, green eyes concealed behind a pair of aviator shades. Aaron dropped Kaleigh's hand and ran to give Jackson a bear hug around the knees.

"Hey, buddy. I'm glad you made it." Jackson shut the cash box labeled "Donations" to return the hug.

His basketball jersey was sleeveless. *As if you need to show off your muscles any more.*

Throwing disdain over discomfort usually worked to cool Kaleigh's blazes of emotion, but this time, she wasn't so sure it would.

Kaleigh handed Jackson three cans out of her backpack, rolling her shoulders after she shed the extra weight.

"Thanks. You didn't have to bring anything." Jackson slid the vegetables toward Mariana, who was seated beside him, taking inventory.

"No problem." At Jackson's other side, Kaleigh noticed Ava working the cotton candy machine. She looked effortlessly adorable as usual in a soft graphic tee with a pumpkin spice latte printed on it. Wisps of spun sugar rested like a crown on top of her caramel-colored bun.

Jackson must have been crazy to give her up for me, Kaleigh thought, but her jealousy was tempered as a stocky guy arrived and planted a kiss on Ava's cheek. The two of them looked smitten.

Kaleigh turned to Jackson to gage his reaction, but he seemed to not even notice. Instead, he started telling Aaron all about the festival's offerings. "And we can get your face painted." He looked to Kaleigh. "If it's okay with your mom."

So, you did hear my request to respect my boundaries. She nodded slightly. "We'll see."

"I'd be happy to take him, since I brought the whole subject up," Jackson said. "The stand is right over there." He pointed across the main thoroughfare, where an artist was set up in plain sight.

Aaron looked at her hopefully. She relented. "All right."

Jackson turned to Mariana. "Are you guys good?"

"Yeah, go ahead." She smiled.

Aaron cheered. "I've never had my face painted before!"

"Then it's about time you have." Jackson put a hand behind his back and led him over. Kaleigh saw Aaron scan through all the pictures pasted to the artist's easel before settling on a tiger face.

His expression of delight as the painter streaked his face with black and orange paint struck Kaleigh with mixed feelings of joy and fear.

Her mind told her, *he's getting too attached to Jackson.* And her heart added in, *Aaron isn't the only one.*

As a child, Lana had exposed Kaleigh to dozens of horrible boyfriends. Kaleigh had determined back then never to do the same to her child. Lana always claimed to be controlling her situation by finding a man to provide for them, but her life's result told a different story. That, along with Kaleigh's own bad relationships, had led her to only one conclusion: staying away from guys altogether was the safest choice.

Yet, she knew Aaron wanted to see another guy in his life, even if he wouldn't complain to her about it. She never wanted to deprive Aaron of any friend or experience.

But if things go South... Ava's boyfriend interrupted Kaleigh's game of mental ping-pong when he extended his hand. "Hi. I'm Pete Harrison."

"Kaleigh Taylor." She accepted the handshake.

"You're the one who's looking for an elementary school?"

"I am. How did you know?"

"Jackson talked to me about your situation." He rubbed his head self-consciously. "Sorry, I thought he would have mentioned it to you by now. Anyway, I work at Citrus Grove Elementary, and I just got the confirmation from my boss yesterday. As long as you fall under our district lines, we'll have a space for your son at our school next year."

Kaleigh's mouth went dry. "We live in the Bella Vista Apartment Complex."

"Oh yeah, we have a few students from there. Have you seen our campus?"

She nodded numbly. "I thought it was a private school."

He produced a packet from the messenger bag at his side. "I brought you an application, if you're interested."

If I'm interested? Grateful tears pricked the back of Kaleigh's eyes. In a daze, she took the application, sat next to Mariana, and wrote her son's name at the top. It seemed like she was endorsing a million-dollar check in their name, instead of filling out a standard kindergarten entry form. "Thank you. This means a lot."

"Don't mention it. I'll be happy to see," Pete glanced at the top of the handout, "Aaron around campus next year."

A tiny roar interrupted her paperwork, and Aaron stood before her with his fingers formed into claws, as pleased as could be. Kaleigh put a hand to her chest. "Don't sneak up on me like that! I thought you were a real tiger!" Aaron laughed at the thought that he had scared his mother.

Ava presented Aaron with a gigantic bag of grape cotton candy and told Jackson, "Seriously, we've got too many people here. You guys go enjoy the festival."

Kaleigh carefully folded the school application for storage in her backpack. She caught Jackson's eye.

"Thank you," she said, trying to communicate in those two words just how much she meant it. *This is everything.*

Kaleigh didn't want to say more to him now in front of Aaron, because this was almost too good to be true, and she was afraid something might fall through with the application. Even if it did, Kaleigh appreciated Jackson's effort.

He had listened to her needs, and then gone out of his way to try and fulfill them. The more that she thought about it, the more Kaleigh wondered if she'd been wrong about him all along.

Even now, she half-expected a quick quip, but he only returned her smile and said, "You're welcome." Jackson turned to Aaron. "So, what do you want to do now?"

Aaron threw his arms in the air and shouted, "The hayride!"

"The hayride it is."

They walked past jewelry makers, spice sellers, grill masters, and carpenters before they reached the City of Summer Shores' big blue tent, where they sold the hayride tickets.

"Can I get yours?" Jackson asked.

Kaleigh shook her head this time and bought tickets for herself and Aaron.

They waited at the end of the line designated for the eleven o'clock departure. When the tractor pulled up, the families in front of them all piled in. By the time Kaleigh, Jackson, and Aaron reached the front, there was only a small space left on the trailer.

The woman loading the passengers asked, "Can you guys squeeze together, or do you want to wait for the next ride?"

Aaron had already danced around in line for twenty minutes and would be disappointed if they had come so close only to not get on. Kaleigh glanced at Jackson, who shrugged his shoulders.

"Sure," she sighed, leading the way up the plywood boards. She sidled in beside a grandma, who was sweating it out in a long-sleeved Jack-o'-lantern shirt.

Jackson guided Aaron up the makeshift ramp next. When he settled his athletic frame down next to hers, their sides connected from shoulder to ankle.

Kaleigh swallowed, pretending to be unaffected. She reached out to pull Aaron onto her lap, but Aaron asked, "Mommy, is it okay if I sit with Jackson?"

"Okay." She faked a smile. "Now that he took you to get face paint, I guess you two are best buds."

Aaron nodded and settled into Jackson's lap. The sight they made cut Kaleigh even deeper than her and Jackson's awkward physical contact.

As Jackson wrapped his long arms around Aaron protectively, it opened up an aching place in Kaleigh that she didn't know was still there.

It's nice to have someone else holding Aaron, and making him smile, she reflected. For once, Kaleigh could breathe—she could lean against the metal railing and enjoy the scenery instead of worrying about Aaron falling through the slats, or Aaron not having a good enough time. However, the wave of exhaustion which slapped over her resting limbs terrified her.

She always kept moving, if nothing else but to keep her functioning. It was the only way to stay strong, to survive on her own. But today, she wasn't on her own, and she had no idea how to act.

Kaleigh knew she couldn't keep condemning Jackson for every little thing, pretending as if she wasn't enjoying their time together. He was in their lives for the time being. Still, she didn't want to be caught unawares. Jackson might very well repeat history and find a more interesting girl to chase.

Then Kaleigh would be Ava, with no Pete waiting for her down the yellow-brick-road. Aaron would be devastated.

Kaleigh cursed every rock in the dirt road that sent her flying against Jackson's shoulder, but, as usual, he was taking it in good humor. Especially when, in an effort to scoot farther away from him, the grandma to her right shot her a stern look and snatched her orange plastic purse away.

Kaleigh's gut reaction was to resist sharing in his laughter, and squelch down the feeling of lightness that threatened to bubble up as she watched Aaron point out orange trees and blueberry bushes, but she didn't want to.

Aaron's brown eyes sparkled with a carelessness he didn't wear enough. And, whether she liked it or not, he was this happy because of Jackson. Jackson pulled Kaleigh out of her shell and made her brave enough to come out here today. Jackson took the time to make Aaron adore him. And she was getting tired of pushing people away.

Today is a good day, Kaleigh reasoned, *and I should enjoy good days when they come around.* Even after Jackson left, she wanted to hold this memory close. She hoped she could give Aaron a hundred more memories like it.

* * *

Jackson had been on much smoother vehicles than this rickety trailer, which seemed determined to throw them off like a bucking bronco. But the feeling of satisfaction that flooded through him as Aaron rested his head against his chest, and as Kaleigh's furrowed brow seemed to relax, was like nothing he'd ever experienced.

Kaleigh's hair hung loose today, like sheets of fire whipping in the wind. She kept fussing at it, trying to smooth it off her face, but the wilder look suited her. And just when he thought that Kaleigh couldn't get more beautiful.

This was what he had been craving—a true connection. A relationship. *A family?*

Where did that come from? Jackson thought. Family had always been a dirty word to him. But maybe if he could find someone to stick by him, it wouldn't have to be anymore.

"What's that in the water?" Aaron yelled as they passed a small pond. The center of the water rippled as something dark and bumpy slithered through.

"That," their driver hollered over the roar of the tractor, "is an alligator." Their fellow passengers gasped and clamored to get a picture. Aaron also leaned forward, gripping the sides of Jackson's arms.

As the water disappeared from their view, cornstalks appeared on the trailer's other side. Jackson craned his neck back to get a better view. The movement brought him even closer to Kaleigh, so close that he caught a whiff of fresh apples. *From her soap, maybe?*

He shook his head and shifted farther into the iron grate on his left, not wanting to make her uncomfortable.

The farmers had built a scarecrow in front of the corn field, with its stuffed arm uplifted to the passengers as they whizzed by.

Kaleigh leaned over and whispered, "Those girls across from us are totally checking you out."

"What?" He whipped his head around. Sure enough, a pair of young women whispered and giggled behind their hands. A few weeks ago, their attention may have stoked Jackson's pride, but now, he wished they would quit.

"I'm sure you've noticed this happens with pretty much everyone who sees you," Kaleigh added.

Not with everyone, Jackson thought.

"They're probably talking about whether or not I'm your sister," she said, rubbing her freckled arms.

Jackson regarded her then. *Is she seriously jealous?* he thought. *Doesn't she know how gorgeous she is?*

Kaleigh would have guys lined up for miles if she stopped giving death glares to anyone who came close enough. But Jackson had stayed close. And now, those glares came less and less frequently.

He guessed that Aaron could also be a deterrent for guys who were interested in Kaleigh. *But that's their loss,* he thought. *Aaron is definitely, definitely a plus.*

Jackson simply replied, "Maybe they are interested in me. But don't worry. They're also not you."

He had once again rendered her speechless, but he didn't comment on it. He didn't want to ruin the tranquil ride by prodding Kaleigh's temper.

Instead, he sighed, completely satisfied as the motion of the trailer whipped up a refreshing breeze. "This was a good idea, buddy," he told Aaron, who beamed.

"Yeah, it was. We should hang out again. And not at that stinky hospital."

Jackson cocked his head. "What did you have in mind?"

"I want to see your house!"

"Aaron!" Kaleigh gasped. "You can't just invite yourself over to people's houses."

"It's fine," Jackson said. "I'd like to have you guys over."

"I'll have to think about it," Kaleigh hedged.

"Aww," Aaron cried.

"Listen to your mom, she has the final say," Jackson told him. He whispered to Kaleigh, "I'll text you my address in case you want to come over on your day off Monday."

She crossed her arms. "Would you please stop stalking me?"

"Hey, the schedules Jenny posts are public information."

Kaleigh just shook her head at that.

The hayride finished its circuit around the property, and everyone stood, brushing pieces of straw from their clothing.

"I guess you should get back to your table," Kaleigh told Jackson.

"The shift I signed up for is over now, if you wanted to stay a while before you have to close the store tonight."

Kaleigh's eyes were daggers.

"What? I can't help it if I have a good memory."

She looked around. "Well, there does seem to be more to do."

Jackson nodded solemnly. "Where to first?"

"I'm hungry." Aaron rubbed his belly.

His mother rolled her eyes. "After all that cotton candy?"

Aaron's resulting grin was tinted purple. "Yep!"

They meandered to a barbecue stand where they ordered pulled pork sandwiches, pop, and chips. Aaron left his sandwich untouched, but happily sipped at his orange drink.

Jackson polished off Aaron's discarded entrée, which was juicy, smoky, and tender.

Newly energized, Aaron's next choice was a trip down a massive inflatable slide.

"That looks so epic!" he cried, proving with the grown-up word that Kaleigh's visits to the library had paid off. "Can we go down the slide, Jackson? Please?"

Jackson groaned, thinking about how the inflatable's pink vinyl surface would rub the wash off his custom-made jeans. "All right."

He climbed up the rope ladder behind Aaron, and they waved to Kaleigh at the top.

The worker at the slide's base hollered, "He's got to ride down with you," and Jackson nodded.

Aaron's little heels kicked Jackson's kneecaps as he squealed in delight all the way down. Kaleigh met them at the bottom, applauding vigorously.

Jackson pulled Aaron up and clapped a hand on his shoulder. "Great job, buddy. You were so brave."

"Again," Aaron pleaded, tugging on the hem of Jackson's jersey.

They zoomed down five more times until Kaleigh put a stop to it. "Come on, take it easy. Jackson'll never get his balance back if you guys don't quit."

But Jackson hadn't minded. Truth be told, this was shaping up to be the best day he'd ever had.

His euphoria made him brave as he walked Kaleigh and Aaron back to their car. After Kaleigh buckled the drowsy kid in the backseat, Jackson couldn't help but lean close and whisper, "Please come over Monday."

Kaleigh straightened and looked into his eyes for a long time, her own eyes unusually vulnerable. Conflicted. *Could she be feeling this magnetism too?* he wondered.

She let out a breath, and Jackson waited for the rejection. Instead, Kaleigh said, "Okay."

Kaleigh spoke just the one word before she hurried into the driver's seat and drove away.

Jackson watched the vehicle pass out of sight before punching his fist in the air. "Yes! Thank you, God."

Maybe after hanging out at church twice a week, his new friends' God-speak was rubbing off on him, but Jackson had to celebrate the "yes" he thought would never happen. He would show Kaleigh that her trust in him was not a mistake.

He texted D'Angelo that he was ready to go. He sent a second text to Isaac: "Solomon knows what he's talking about."

8

Jackson's nerves were shot by the time Monday rolled around. His apartment was impeccably clean, with no dirty shorts in sight. He'd borrowed a bottle of cinnamon-scented room spray from Miss Lewis and spritzed it all around.

Duke whimpered pitifully from inside Jackson's bedroom. His dog was unused to such treatment, but Jackson didn't want Aaron to be surprised by a big brute charging him at the door.

On his white marble kitchen island, a collection of animal crackers, orange pop bottles, and candy rested alongside a fruit tray (in case Kaleigh nixed the junk food). He wanted to be a good host, and remembered how Aaron loved snacks, but he hoped Kaleigh wouldn't think this was too over-the-top.

Finally, his phone buzzed with a text from Kaleigh, saying, "We're here."

Jackson strode out of his apartment—choosing to jog down the stairs and release some of his nervous energy instead of taking the elevator—and hurried toward the building's front door. He could see Kaleigh and Aaron approaching through the glass.

Kaleigh'd straightened her hair, and she wore a flattering blue V-neck tee. She made cargo capris and strappy sandals look designer. He swallowed and shoved the door open. "Hey, guys."

Aaron burst out, "This is the best house ever!" He bounced on the toes of his superhero shoes.

"Thanks," Jackson chuckled. "My apartment's upstairs. I was hoping someone could push the elevator button for me..."

"I will, I will!" Aaron ran ahead to prove that he was up for the task.

They passed through the luxurious lobby and piled in the elevator. Jackson looked for Kaleigh's reaction, but she was quiet, studying their surroundings. They exited to his floor's long hall.

After a quick glance at the ceiling, she said, "Hmm. I guess whoever designed this complex must have decided that one chandelier wasn't enough."

"It is a little much, isn't it?" Jackson said, though he had never thought about it before now. From childhood, he was used to staying in nice hotels whenever his dad had a convention for work, and his childhood home had as many floors as the building they were standing in.

Jackson keyed into his apartment, wanting to get through the entryway as quickly as possible, but Kaleigh slowed in the threshold. She eyed the small abstract sculptures on the glass tables which had been included when he signed his lease. He prayed she wouldn't notice that they were originals.

"I hope we don't mess anything up." She crossed her arms.

"No, don't worry about that. It's usually a mess, honestly. I just wanted to make sure it looked nice for you."

"Well, I'm sure if Aaron knocks something over, it would be easy enough for you to replace it."

"That's right," Jackson said, slightly unnerved by her cool tone. "Anyway, the kitchen's through here." He threw his hand over his shoulder and led the way.

The snack collection did put a smile on Kaleigh's face. Jackson's shoulders sagged in relief.

"Are all these for us?" Aaron asked.

"They sure are."

"Mommy, can I get some?"

"Go ahead."

While his fingers curled around a bag of crackers, he asked, "Can I get more than one thing?"

"Oh, just get what you'd like. Today's a special occasion."

"Hooray, two special eggcations in one week!" Aaron said. He fisted a chocolate bar, tucked a pop under his arm, and ran to the the living room.

Kaleigh put some grapes for herself on a paper plate before following. "Thanks for this," she told Jackson.

"Don't mention it."

"That's the biggest TV I ever saw!" Aaron shouted, having already plopped down on the couch.

Kaleigh winced at the sight of his bottle of pop sloshing up and down in his hand. "Here, honey, let me open that for you."

Meanwhile, Aaron put his finger on the glowing recliner button, and watched the legs of the sofa extend. "I have powers," he whispered reverently.

After this statement, Jackson and Kaleigh kept their laughter quiet, not wanting to spoil his fun.

Kaleigh sat down next to Aaron, and Jackson lowered himself next to her. Her eyes passed over the '90s family flick Jackson had found to stream on the flat-screen.

"Wow, that's a blast from the past."

Jackson ran his fingers over the top of his coiffure. "I wasn't sure what shows kids like nowadays, but I figured this was safe enough."

He vaguely remembered the movie's storyline from his own childhood—a little girl ran away from home to enjoy adventures in the big city. Aaron seemed enthralled.

"What do you normally watch?" Kaleigh asked Jackson.

"Hockey."

That got Aaron's attention. "Hockey?"

Jackson shrugged. "Yeah. I used to play a little. If you're okay with dogs, in a minute, I'll run to my room and bring out my college trophies." Duke was scratching the bedroom door anyway—it would be nice to let him free. Really, though, Jackson didn't want to invite them to see and then have to explain the luggage pushed beside his bed.

"I love dogs!"

"Good." Jackson leaned back and crossed his arms behind his head. "I was a decent hockey player. Actually, I was scouted for the pros, but my dad didn't think sports was a serious enough career."

"So, if hockey's over, what are you going to do now?" Kaleigh asked.

The question took his breath away. *Calm down,* Jackson told himself. *It's not as if she knows about Costa Rica...* "I guess I'm just looking to try something different."

"It must be nice to float around without a plan," Kaleigh bit her lip and then glanced at Aaron. In a lower tone, she said, "Sorry. I'm trying to not be so harsh to people." She shrugged her shoulder. "I've worked hard to get where I'm at, and now the hard work is paying off."

"Was being a PTA always the plan?"

Kaleigh laughed. "Ironically, I was thinking about pro sports too. I wanted to be an athletic trainer for soccer players, if I couldn't cut it as an athlete myself."

"What happened—" he trailed off, looking at Aaron.

She smiled. "Fate had better things in mind."

"Or God did."

Kaleigh's mouth puckered. "Anyway. Do you still skate?"

"I do. I have to drive a little farther than I'm used to, but there's a rink thirty miles from here. We should go sometime."

Kaleigh scoffed. "Ice skating?"

"Yeah," he said. "All three of us."

A bark came from his bedroom and Jackson hopped to his feet. "Stay here, okay, buddy?" he told Aaron.

Jackson opened the door slightly and wrapped an arm around Duke.

The dog fairly dragged him to the couch in his eagerness to greet their visitors.

Aaron leapt off his seat with equal excitement, and Duke licked Aaron's hands happily. The kid screamed in laughter, yanking his fingers away. After he was sure that Jackson was keeping Duke still, Aaron reached out again to touch the top of Duke's head.

The big ham of a dog collapsed to the floor so he could get a belly rub, too, sticking his paws in the air. His tongue lolled out of his mouth as he cocked his head and looked at Aaron expectantly.

After that, Aaron had eyes for nothing else—not even Jackson's magical couch. The two fast friends hung out on the floor together for the rest of the visit.

He liked this laid-back version of Aaron, who usually seemed so reserved for an almost-five-year-old boy. Jackson seemed to be making strides with both Aaron and his mom.

He knew he would have to tell Kaleigh about Costa Rica eventually, but he'd wait until he'd figured out more of the details, like how he could make sure they were cared for while he was away, and how to stop Kaleigh from withdrawing from him. He had let her down before by letting things with Ava drag on too long, and Jackson knew it was unlikely Kaleigh would forgive him if he made a second mistake.

Watching her and Aaron fill his living room with love and laughter, Jackson wanted to keep them just like this.

* * *

Later that afternoon, Jackson met Isaac at the church to prepare for their scheduled food donation drop-off. The town had given generously during the fall fest, and they'd come away with an envelope of cash, plus several weighty boxes of canned goods to deliver to the local charity.

Isaac had his own key to the church, so they quickly entered the quiet building, flipped on the lights, and transferred the boxes from the fellowship hall into the backseat of Isaac's truck.

"Thanks for helping me out." Isaac grunted under the weight of his heavy load.

"No problem," Jackson answered. "That's one benefit of shiftwork. I'm available at different times than anyone else is."

"Tell me about it." Isaac would understand as a work-from-home computer programmer.

After the last box was loaded, they both stepped into the cab. Jackson didn't comment on the country music that blasted out when Isaac turned on the ignition.

They may have come from the same state, but Isaac was a corn-fed Iowan, through and through. Instead, Jackson looked out the window, the Taylors' visit on his mind.

"Something bothering you?" Isaac asked as he pulled the truck out of the church lot. "Is Kaleigh still giving you a hard time?"

"No, we're doing much better, actually. She even agreed to go ice skating with me. There's just one problem."

"What's that?" Isaac regarded him from underneath his curtain of shaggy black bangs.

There is no other way to say this, Jackson thought. Maybe telling Isaac would be good practice for breaking the news to Kaleigh. "I'm scheduled to go to Costa Rica in January."

"Okay," Isaac said slowly. "For a vacation?"

"No. For a year. In high school, my counselor made us take this quiz about the things we'd be good at? All my careers had to do with travel, and I read about people who live overseas and plan activities for the locals. It's been my dream ever since."

"You make it sound almost glamorous. Those I've known who've gone into the mission field had to sacrifice a lot."

"I'm not explaining it well enough...I mean, yeah, I want to do good there. I'd be doing good and helping myself at the same time. What's wrong with that?"

Isaac pressed his lips together. "I'm sure whatever group you're going with has people who change their mind all the time. What happens if you turn them down?"

"There's no real penalty, but I wouldn't get accepted a second time."

"And, you're not sure that you want to stay here."

"I want to stay," Jackson pressed his temple against the window. "I'm just not sure that, if I do, I won't have any regrets. I'm finally making progress with Kaleigh, so I can't be on the fence with my commitment. It wouldn't be fair. I need to be sure."

"Maybe she'd wait for you to finish."

"Now that I know more about her responsibilities, I'm realizing that I would be asking a lot. When I think about giving up my plans, it feels wrong. But when I think about leaving Kaleigh and Aaron alone, that feels wrong, too."

"I'll keep you in my prayers, man. It can be hard to know what to do sometimes. I'm sure it will all work out."

"Yeah." Jackson had tried to pray too, in a similar way to the verses which Isaac had highlighted in the Bible. But every time he got to "thy will be done," Jackson choked. Was he really prepared to let go of what he wanted, even if Costa Rica wasn't a part of God's plan at all?

Jackson's hands tensed as, through the windshield, he watched a motorcycle zip around a vehicle in the opposite lane. He turned his gaze completely to stare out the side window, still jumpy about watching oncoming traffic after his car accident.

If Isaac noticed, he didn't say anything. He pulled into the backside of a slate-colored warehouse, where a group of teenagers wearing orange vests and black gloves were waiting for them.

Jackson hopped out to assist them in unloading the goods into a gigantic, rolling bin.

An older woman with a clipboard emerged and instructed the volunteers on what foods would go on what shelves inside.

She turned to Isaac, who had rolled his window down. "Would you like the donation weighed for tax purposes?"

"No, that's all right," he said.

Peering in at the distribution center's inventory, Jackson was amazed at how much food the local pantry had amassed.

"How many people do you serve?" Jackson asked the woman.

"Thousands every year," she replied. "They drive in from multiple counties to get food, referrals, or counseling."

"I had no idea." Jackson had signed up to help with the food drive to be a part of a church activity, but now he was happy to be a small part of what was going on there. "How did this all get started, from a government program?"

"No, we do get help from a national organization, but I started this center five years ago. I've been in a place where I needed help, and I wanted to be there for others."

"That's amazing," Isaac said. "Well, it's been great to meet you."

She shook their hands. "And you as well. Thank you for your donation!"

Jackson nodded and got back in the passenger seat.

"Now that's service," Isaac remarked. "You can serve anywhere, if you're thinking of the people more than of yourself."

His comment landed uncomfortably in Jackson's gut, like a wriggling worm. Jackson rubbed the top of his thighs. "I just need some more time to think."

"That's understandable," Isaac said. He pulled down his sun visor and met Jackson's eyes. "Just don't wait too long."

9

Aaron coughed pitifully and swiped his nose with his fist.

"Use a tissue, honey." Kaleigh handed him the box. But Aaron seemed unconcerned with snot bubbles at that moment.

"You have to go skating without me! Mrs. McCauley can babysit. We already talked about how Jackson's your soulmate."

"You know what a soulmate is?"

Aaron nodded solemnly. "We watch a lot of soap operas together."

Oh my. "We're going to have to talk about that later. We'll have to pick another day to hang out with Jackson."

Aaron groaned. "Just ask her, okay, Mommy? You need to take a day off."

The kid was four going on fourteen. "I need to be with my sick child," Kaleigh countered.

"Actually," he articulated slowly, making the word's three syllables sound like four, "Mrs. McCauley knows how to heat up soup, too. I don't even have a fever."

Kaleigh lowered her hand to feel Aaron's forehead again. "Don't you want me to stay with you?"

"The only thing that will make me feel better is if you go with Jackson." Aaron stuck out his lower lip and folded his skinny arms.

Kaleigh didn't want to pay for another hour of babysitting, especially when Aaron had a cold, but she guessed it wouldn't hurt to ask their neighbor. The conniving child really seemed to have his heart set on it.

She had such a hard time deciding how often to tell him "no." Aaron didn't ask for much. But, she was also afraid that when she went and nothing romantic happened, he would be disappointed. Then again, maybe a solo, platonic outing would be just the thing to show him once and for all that she and Jackson were just friends...

"All right, I'll ask. But don't be upset if she says no. She might not want to catch your cold."

Mrs. McCauley replied to Kaleigh's text immediately, expressing that a visit would be just fine. Kaleigh sighed and told Aaron to get his shoes on for the trip across the complex.

Now she'd have to redo her ponytail and change from her mom-survival uniform into a decent outfit. Not that she was looking to impress anyone, of course.

***

One short hour later, Kaleigh grumbled, "I can't believe I let you talk me into this."

She looped the long laces of her brown rental skates into a tight knot. Jackson had already expertly tied his own skates and slipped on his old high school jersey. Though he wore jeans, Kaleigh could picture him all suited up with padding, helmet and all.

His ankles didn't buckle like she feared hers would. In fact, he was hopping from blade to blade with a restless anticipation as he waited for Kaleigh to finish. Although she didn't have to look after Aaron for the afternoon, she got the distinct feeling that she'd still be filling the "responsible adult" role.

"It's good to try new things," Jackson replied, peering through the lobby window to the ice beyond.

"Next time, I'm picking the activity."

Jackson's eyebrows rose, and she realized that she had implied they would see each other again. "If I survive to see another day," she added lamely. She grabbed onto the railing that led into the rink, already wobbling off-ice.

"Here, let me help you." Jackson reached out as if to peel her white-knuckled death grip from the railing.

"No," she said firmly and hobbled her way to the door, opening it to a wave of cold air.

Her fleece quarter-zip pullover and yoga pants seemed too thin now. Jackson snorted as she paused to pull a pair of gloves and earmuffs out of her pockets.

"What, did you leave your parka at home? If we get moving, you won't need any of that."

She glared at him, but still took his arm as she eased onto the ice.

"Try standing taller."

"I hate you," Kaleigh huffed, since all the energy needed for an eloquent response was already engaged in staying upright. She released Jackson to clutch the plexiglass ledge.

Once she was steady, Kaleigh did try to stand straighter. Slowly, she crept forward.

"Have you ever been skating before?" Jackson asked.

"Once, at an outdoor rink with my mom. It was Christmastime."

"You're not a first-timer, then?"

"I was only six. I barely remember going, let alone how to skate." But that wasn't true. She could picture every detail.

She remembered the way that practice skaters flew around the outer edges, just like on TV—twirling, jumping and landing lightly on their feet. She remembered the peppermint hot chocolate she and Lana drank together on the hard wooden benches.

For once, Lana hadn't been grumpy, and she hadn't had a selfish agenda in taking Kaleigh there. Lana'd even shared a rare detail from her childhood—she'd loved skating at Christmastime.

Kaleigh remembered no other time in her own childhood that she had been so happy.

"You're getting better," Jackson said, interrupting her melancholy thoughts. He was skating backwards, slaloming from side to side. "You could probably skate away from the wall now."

"I don't want to fall."

"I won't let you." His hands were an invitation, his eyes a promise. A plea for her to believe him. She wondered if he was talking about skating anymore at all.

Even through her gloves, when their fingers touched, she shivered —but it was from the heat instead of the cold.

Jackson stopped showing off and glided slowly before her, his blades crunching on the smooth ice. "There. That wasn't so hard, was it?"

She shook her head, though her insides were still quaking. He wrapped his hands around her wrists, and the grip proved that he was strong enough to support her. If only she had that kind of confidence in his internal qualities.

"See? You just had to let go and know that someone's here to catch you. Someone who cares about you."

Her insides twisted. Aaron's dad had claimed to care about her, too. He cared, until she discovered she was pregnant. When things got tough, she found out just how un-caring people could be.

"That's a pretty phrase," she bit out. "You should try it on someone who's never fallen."

Jackson considered her words, and then tossed his head in the direction of the bleachers. "Sure. It would be safer if you sat down over there. But what would you be missing?"

Now that she felt more secure in Jackson's grip, Kaleigh turned her attention away from her feet's choppy movements to relish the breeze created from their momentum. The weight of her blades on the ice and his hands under hers were the only things grounding her in reality. Gliding like this, she could almost imagine that she was flying.

Jackson's grip loosened and her eyes snapped wide open. She was skating all by herself! That was, until her toe pick caught in a small dip in the ice. She gasped, arms flailing, and fell forward, right onto Jackson's chest. The impact sent his blades flying out from under him, and he toppled backwards.

His six-pack was not a soft landing space, and her breath left her in a whoosh. But at least his arms had snapped around her and kept her from hitting the ice.

Kaleigh took in the pain in his expression and remembered his therapy session. "Will your knee be okay?"

Jackson grunted. "Yeah. I don't know about my backside, though." He watched her for a breath, and the amusement in his gaze flamed into a fire. But then, he blinked and carefully placed her beside him.

Kaleigh berated herself: *What, did you actually think that he was going to kiss you?*

Jackson stretched, then rose with a groan. Kaleigh did the same, laughing when she saw his wet jeans.

"Are you cold now?" she asked sweetly.

"Not even a little." He grinned. Jackson took just one of her hands this time. She let him without complaint and wondered if more than one best memory would be made in an ice arena.

* * *

"I hope Aaron wasn't too upset he missed out today." Jackson yanked off his skates and swiped the blades with a towel. A sniff of musty air made him think he should have washed his gear before coming out.

He slid his soft, navy soakers on the blades and nestled the skates into his duffel bag. The bag still boasted "11" in white block numerals.

It was funny how a number that had once brought him so much joy and glory became obsolete in a few years' time. If he went back to the Ashwood arena, he doubted that anyone there would recognize him.

"No, Aaron wasn't upset about it being just the two of us," Kaleigh said with an irritation in her voice Jackson didn't understand.

He shrugged it off. "I had a great time, but I feel bad about him lying sick at home. Does he need anything?"

"Nah, at this age, Aaron's a germ magnet. I keep the tissues and soups in stock."

Kaleigh returned her rental skates to the counter, and they meandered toward the building's exit.

A pro shop to their left caught Jackson's eye. "Would you mind if I sent a souvenir home with you?"

Kaleigh bit her lip. "I guess that would be okay."

Jackson swung open the glass door and nodded to the high-school girl flipping through a magazine at the small room's cash register.

Kaleigh ran her fingers appreciatively over bedazzled figure-skating dresses and brightly-hued jackets. Her hand caught a price tag.

"You don't want to look," Jackson said. "Trust me."

She scrunched up her nose and dropped the tag. "You're probably right."

Jackson strolled toward the hockey section. "I usually am."

She rolled her eyes, but he was glad that she'd stopped taking his boasting so seriously. If she only knew how insecure he could get, she would never take it seriously again.

Jackson looked to the jerseys, but then cast his eyes over to the skates. Kaleigh followed his gaze. "No."

"Why not?"

"They're too expensive."

Jackson waved that protest away.

She put her finger up. "And dangerous. I'm not putting him into lessons."

Jackson was already scouring the shelves. "I'll teach him."

Kaleigh slid a hand over her face. "Let's take this slow, all right? We're already spending a lot of time together."

"Take what slow?"

Kaleigh made a strangled noise. "You know. Our friendship."

Jackson nodded. "I'll take it. It's a lot better than you viewing me as your mortal enemy."

She stepped closer. "Need I remind you why I'm tempted to see you that way?"

"No," Jackson said, sobered. Would he ever shake his past?

Kaleigh turned to look at the display. "I wish I could buy things like this for Aaron."

"This?" Jackson threw a hand toward the rows of boxes. "This is nothing compared to the love you give Aaron. You give him everything you have. Take it from someone whose parents were expert gift-givers. The most perfect and expensive presents can't make up for the lack of feeling behind them."

"And," she started slowly, "there's feeling behind this gift?"

Jackson swallowed, casting a glance at the teenager whose magazine pages had stopped flipping. This wasn't exactly the place he would have chosen to pour his heart out, but he was afraid Kaleigh wouldn't give him another opportunity if he stayed silent now.

His eyes met her blue ones, shining like twin raindrops in her heart-shaped face. "It holds more feeling than I've ever felt before."

The air between them crackled. Time slowed, until the cashier popped her bubble gum. Kaleigh and Jackson pivoted toward her, and she hurriedly stuck her face back in her reading material.

Jackson scratched the back of his head. "So," he drew out the word. "Would something like this work?"

He tapped a display skate. It was black, shot with neon-green stripes.

"Aaron would love it," she admitted. "Do they have a kids size eleven?"

Jackson pulled a ten out of the middle of the stack. "We're in luck. You always want your skates to fit tighter than your normal size."

A wave of nostalgia rolled over him as he recalled getting his first pair of skates. Though they may not have been as thoughtfully chosen, the hockey lessons which his parents paid for were the road to countless happy days. Days filled with rambunctious kids, and encouraging adults. Jackson would sweat out his frustration and have something positive to put his energy towards.

He was lucky his father's interest in perfection didn't extend from his work to sports, or else Marcus probably would have taught Jackson to hate hockey too.

Kaleigh folded her arms and faced the door while the employee rang up Jackson's purchase. He quickly checked the racks of gear for extra-smalls and added a helmet, padding, and bag to the pile, wiping out the store's meager youth section.

Kaleigh peeked back at the register. "What's all this?"

"For safety." She could hardly argue with that.

Although Jackson was happy to provide the equipment for Aaron, he would have to find a way to give Kaleigh something that wasn't monetary. Jackson couldn't assume that the way his parents had always shown their "love" would work with anyone else. After all, it hadn't worked on him.

Only one thing came to mind. He recalled the days when his nonna would bustle around her son's sterile kitchen and tsk, addressing the air in place of her absent child. "Oh, Marcus. Food should be messy. Colorful. Joyful."

Jackson's father was always working during her visits. But that fact didn't sting as much when Nonna started pulling ingredients for butter cookies out of her canvas bag.

The warmth she created didn't come from the preheated oven. Though her cooking was a simple act, it was more the time and effort she put in that made an impact on Jackson. The fact someone had thought of him.

Isaac's voice came to Jackson's mind, encouraging him to try persisting through hard tasks. The learning curve for hosting Aaron and Kaleigh for a meal might be painful, but Jackson knew that was what he had to do.

10

A few minutes into their next shared shift, Jackson slapped his hands down on either side of Kaleigh's register. "Don't worry, I'm here."

Kaleigh startled and dropped the receipt paper she'd been loading into the printer. The roll unfurled in a long line, all the way across the room.

"Sorry," he said. "I didn't mean to scare you."

"I know." *What is wrong with me?* Kaleigh thought. She shouldn't turn into a klutz just because Jackson was around.

"Green," Jenny barked. "You're late. I need you to work the other end of the store." The manager then turned her gaze to Kaleigh, who was standing with fingers still outstretched from where the roll had been. "Are you going to clean this up?"

Kaleigh shook her head free of the cobwebs. "Of course." She hurried to the work.

Jenny wasn't usually so curt, but Jackson had been distracting Kaleigh more often when they worked together. He'd have to be careful, or he'd be called into the office next.

Mariana walked out of the stockroom and nearly tripped over the discarded receipt roll. "Kaleigh? Oh, here, let me help you." She picked up the plastic core and started winding the paper back into place.

"Thanks," Kaleigh answered, returning to the register to pick up the opposite end.

"No problem." Mariana tossed her head to force her waist-length curls back over her shoulder.

"Good thing we haven't opened for the day."

Mariana handed the replenished roll to Kaleigh and huffed. "I'm not a fan of early shifts, but Ava roped me into going to this library sale later, so I had to free up my afternoon."

"Really? I was thinking of going to that sale too."

"I'm not a reader, but Ava needs to build up her classroom library. I'm just coming for moral support. You should meet us there."

"Oh." Kaleigh swallowed hard. "I'm actually going with my son."

Mariana gasped. "That's great! I'd love to meet your son."

"He's going to hang out in the kids' section and want to look at every DVD."

"Kaleigh, it's fine! Unless you guys would rather spend time just the two of you?"

"Actually, it's always just the two of us. Aaron might like being a part of a bigger group for a change."

"Perfect. We should be there around two."

"Sounds good," Kaleigh said, though she wasn't so sure.

* * *

Seven hours later, and the Taylors were bumping elbows with what must have been fifty of Summer Shores' book lovers. It had been a miracle they'd been able to spot Mariana and Ava across the overflowing crowd in the community library.

It'd been awkward for Kaleigh to see Ava ever since Jackson had flirted with Kaleigh, upset the girl, and left her crying at Hydrangea. Kaleigh hadn't meant to interfere with their relationship—she hadn't even known about it—but the workplace drama left her feeling guilty all the same.

Yet, Ava was clearly over it. She hadn't acted weird last time she saw Kaleigh at the fall fest.

Now, Ava and Mariana were making a big show over Aaron's book sale choices: a board book about construction vehicles, some seek-and-find titles, and a few classic children's stories that Kaleigh found.

"That's so good for him, you know," Ava whispered to Kaleigh. "To start reading to him this young."

"I hope so." It was hard to feel threatened by Ava when she was being so nice.

"Thanks for being good sports and supporting my book-buying habit." Ava's thin arms strained under the weight of her near-full cardboard box.

"*Enabling* your book-buying habit is more like it. Nerd," Mariana teased. Despite her complaints, she'd scouted out a few cookbooks to take home.

"This is exactly why we need reading," Ava sniffed. "A person can improve her mind and learn to use her words for good and not evil."

Kaleigh laughed, too caught up in the silly exchange to remember not to draw attention to herself.

"Do you want to look around some more, Kaleigh?" Ava asked.

"Well..." Kaleigh peeked at Aaron, who was flipping through Mari's new recipes.

"It's okay, Mommy. You can go," he said.

"All right," Kaleigh told Ava. "Thanks."

Kaleigh chose a few thrillers which looked promising, and an old physical therapy textbook. When she saw Aaron was still occupied with his two new friends, she couldn't resist taking one last pass through the kids' section. She was rewarded with a Pre-Kindergarten workbook in decent condition.

Once they brought their hauls to the checkout line, Aaron turned to Kaleigh. "Why didn't Jackson come?"

Kaleigh's cheeks flushed. "I didn't invite him. He doesn't have to go everywhere we go."

"But I like when he comes places with us."

"Aren't you having fun?"

"Mm-hmm!" he said, swinging two of his books under his arms.

After a beat of silence, Ava casually said, "I think Jackson's really changed since his accident."

"Oh?" Kaleigh studied the workbook's creased spine.

"He comes to church twice a week. And he's not just floating through. He's been pitching in at service events, trying to learn during Bible study..."

"Learn what?" Kaleigh asked, in spite of herself. She was intrigued by this picture of Jackson, the scholar.

"What Jesus did for us, and how to live now that we know it. You should come by and see for yourself!"

"I don't think so." Kaleigh smirked. "The roof might collapse if I step inside."

"Don't be silly. We'd love to have you and Aaron come."

"Thanks for the invitation."

Sustaining the light tone appropriate for a cordial afternoon out had been a change for Kaleigh. The venom in her last comment, however, slammed the door on further conversation, and fit her voice as comfortably as her favorite pair of knit gloves.

The memory of her senior classmates staring at her swollen belly hadn't left Kaleigh's mind easily. How much worse would the gossip be behind the doors of place dedicated to holiness?

Ava and Mariana had been supportive today, but church was not a part of Kaleigh's plan.

* * *

Aaron didn't have to wait long to see Jackson again—as soon as Kaleigh'd driven home from the library sale, a text came in from Jackson, asking to set up Aaron's first private lesson for the following day.

In the warming house of the rink, it had taken a full twenty minutes to unbox and put on all the new hockey gear.

"Are you sure all this is necessary?" Kaleigh asked, pursing her lips.

Starkly framed by the entrance to the white ice, Aaron looked like a dark foam hockey monster had swallowed him up. Only his chocolate eyes were visible through his face mask.

"He needs to get used to the weight of the gear if he's ever going to learn properly."

"Where's my stick?" Aaron asked.

"You don't need one yet. Lesson one is how to stand."

"I know how to stand, silly."

"Not on ice, you don't." Jackson bent down and put a hand on Aaron's shoulders. "Don't you want to learn how to be a star hockey player?"

Kaleigh cleared her throat.

Jackson rolled his eyes. "And learn how to have fun and make friends with the other players?"

"Yeah!"

"Then you've got to listen to your coach."

Aaron grinned at the word "coach," and nodded.

Jackson rubbed his hands together. "All right, then. Parents to the stands!"

It was difficult to walk away, but it wasn't as if Kaleigh would be much help on the ice anyway. It was funny—the other day, Jackson had described the bleachers as a place of safety, but Kaleigh felt more helpless watching Aaron than she did skating herself.

But Jackson kept his hands wrapped around Aaron's armpits, and her little guy was soon taking choppy strides down the ice.

Skating backwards, Jackson showed Aaron how to angle his blade to gain more power. Much to Kaleigh's surprise, the next thing Jackson did was to lead Aaron to the center of the rink and ease him down to his backside. Then, he plopped down beside him, demonstrating how to crawl up on all fours.

Jackson did a decent imitation of Duke, howling at other public session skaters and wagging his tongue. Aaron joined in with delight.

Jackson helped Aaron kneel, pick one foot up, and then the other to return to a standing position. Next, he put their backs against the plexiglass and pretended to squat down and eat a meal.

Kaleigh didn't see how Aaron was going to learn anything if he kept on giggling. But they practiced "eating" again and again, keeping their shoulders back.

They pushed off the side and skated a few strides forward on their own, with Jackson modeling how to move his arms backward and forward. Jackson gently lifted Aaron's chin when he kept looking at his feet until, eventually, Aaron's stance improved. When Aaron successfully replicated the proper technique, Jackson slapped his hand with a big high five.

It was a half-hour before Aaron started to lose focus, dancing around and scraping circles in the ice instead of listening to "coach." *Snack time*, Kaleigh guessed, and she met them back at the entrance.

"You did so well!" she told Aaron.

He beamed and ran ahead to the warming house. She and Jackson followed, side by side. The heat inside the room prickled Kaleigh's chilled skin painfully, but she was more concerned with the attraction swelling in her chest like a physical force.

Seeing this big, sometimes lazy man turn all the power of his attention on her little guy had been absolutely heart-wrenching. As flustered as she was, she neglected to argue with him about buying their pizzas and sodas at the concession stand. Instead, they carried their food in peace and sat at a hard plastic table.

"Did you see me, Mommy?" Aaron asked. "I didn't fall down once!"

"I saw. That was better than I did in my ice skating lesson." Kaleigh's cheeks flamed at the memory of how that lesson had ended.

"It's okay, you just need some more practice."

"You're right as usual, my little wise guy." Kaleigh gently pinched his cheek.

"Do you guys mind if I ask a blessing over the food?" Jackson asked.

"Oh, um...sure." Kaleigh motioned for Aaron to fold his hands and close his eyes, since she was sure he had never seen anyone pray before.

"Dear God," Jackson's voice quavered, and he took a deep breath. "Thank you for our time here today. Please bless this food to our bodies. In Jesus's name, Amen." His voice had seemed to get quicker the closer he got to the end of the prayer.

"That was short," Aaron remarked. Kaleigh bumped his knee under the table and shook her head.

Jackson smiled. "I guess I just need some more practice, too."

Aaron blew on his pizza slice. "When you talk to God, does He really listen?"

"Yes, I think so."

"And you can ask Him for anything?"

"Sure."

Aaron grinned. "I know what I'm going to ask Him for."

Kaleigh could imagine what he was referring to. She interjected, "So, Jackson, when did you start skating?"

"When I was about Aaron's age." He sipped on his soda and launched into the full history.

Kaleigh was glad the topic had shifted away from prayer, but it had been nice to learn that Jackson wasn't comfortable doing everything. Sometimes, with all his bluster, he made it seem like he was.

Now Jackson was letting them close enough to see his vulnerabilities along with his skills, which added to the intoxicating suspicion that he was someone she was right to put her faith in.

So, when he invited them to his apartment for a home-cooked dinner, at the sight of Aaron's glowing face, and Jackson's hopeful one, it was an easier "yes" to give.

11

Jackson spent Friday poring over Nonna's recipe book. He'd never been one to cook over ordering out, and didn't have the nerve to attempt one of her signature dishes, as she'd hand-penciled the directions on note cards with vague instructions like "toss in a pinch of oregano."

Finally, he settled on an online recipe for fettuccini alfredo that didn't have too many steps.

Nonna had called the pasta "Italian-American food," but she made it often enough for Jackson as a little boy. She'd offered to show him how to make it, but he'd been too lazy at the time.

If he could go back, he would have paid attention, washed dishes, done anything if he could be with his warmest, wisest family member again. Now, he only hoped he could remember a few of her techniques.

D'Angelo chauffeured Jackson to the supermarket, where he picked up mozzarella and prosciutto for an appetizer, and flour, eggs, parmigiano, butter, and shallots for the pasta.

He knew he had olive oil. Though Jackson was no chef, Nonna never would have forgiven him for leaving his pantry bare of that.

The girl at the checkout counter raised her eyebrows when she rang up the brand-new stand mixer with pasta-making implement, but Jackson didn't blink at the total.

Back home, he got so worried about messing something up that he called Miss Lewis to enlist her to help with the meal. Even so, Jackson was surprised at how enjoyable the tasks turned out to be, like rolling out dough with his own hands and smelling the aromatic shallots as he whirled them around in oil. It reminded him of a science experiment, getting the consistency of the dough and the sauce just right.

Miss Lewis insisted on supervising instead of taking over the "hard stuff" that wasn't so hard after all—just new. She was nuking Aaron's favorite chicken nuggets in the microwave when she struck up a conversation.

"You know, D'Angelo took me on a trip to Daytona last weekend. I was surprised, since he drives every day for his job, but he said that he enjoyed every mile. We had a nice picnic on the beach. I don't suppose you had anything to do with that?" Miss Lewis shot him a knowing look.

"Of course not." Jackson'd helped plan the whole thing. He had a way of creating romantic moments, even if D'Angelo had shot down his brilliant dancing-class idea.

She straightened the collar of Jackson's peach polo. "You're all right, kid. By the way, I found a new position. Are you sure that you're leaving town?"

"I'm not sure of anything," Jackson muttered.

The microwave timer beeped, and she pulled the steaming plate out by its edges. "You seem different now than you did since you first came here. Happier. More settled."

"I am, but..." How could he explain why he couldn't settle yet?

They both turned to the sound of a sharp rapping on the apartment door. Jackson held his hands up. "Please don't say anything to Kaleigh."

The housekeeper nodded but pursed her lips in disapproval.

Duke added to the knocking noise with barking, reminding Jackson to grab his leather collar before swinging the door open.

Kaleigh wore her hair down straight tonight. It tickled the base of her bare collarbones as she fiddled with the skirt of her sleeveless dress. Cotton, the color of melted butterscotch, floated out from her trim waist and bunched underneath her fingers.

"We're here," she stated the obvious.

"You look amazing," Jackson said, and immediately regretted it.

Idiot. She doesn't like it when you compliment her.

But Kaleigh's lips just curved into a tiny smile. She tucked her hair behind her ears. "Can we come in?"

"Of course." He stepped aside.

She sniffed. "It smells good in here."

"Do you like Italian?"

"I love it."

Jackson exhaled. "I hope you still do when you leave. Please, have a seat."

He leaned down to Duke and said, "Behave yourself," making sure that Aaron was safe on the couch before letting the mutt loose to cover the tyke in wet kisses.

Miss Lewis appeared with the meat and cheese dish. "Aaron!"

During the Taylors' last visit, Jackson had discovered that the typically-stalwart housekeeper had a major soft spot for little ones. She dropped the dish down on the end table. "Do you want to take Duke out for a walk while your nuggets cool down?"

Jackson couldn't help but glance at Kaleigh, whose eyes were glued to the floor. It looked like Miss Lewis was trying to pay him back for setting her up with D'Angelo.

"Yeah! Can I, Mommy?"

Kaleigh swallowed. "Sure."

"Let me get you something to drink." Jackson wasn't usually flustered around women, but somehow seeing her there on his couch in the fading daylight felt much different than skating together in a public session or hanging out with Aaron.

She fairly had to shout after him as he rushed into the kitchen. "Do you have Dr. Pepper?"

"I do," he hollered back, already popping the tab and pouring the liquid into a crystal glass. He'd noticed that Kaleigh always bought a bottle of Dr. Pepper mid-shift from the break room vending machine.

By the time Jackson took a steadying breath and re-emerged in the living room, Aaron and Miss Lewis were gone.

If he would've sat on the armchair catty-cornered from her perch on the couch, it would've felt awkwardly far away, so Jackson slowly took a seat beside Kaleigh. He offered her the glass, anchoring his elbow on his knee to keep it from shaking. Their fingers brushed, and

Kaleigh's voice was breathy when she said, "Thank you."

The thick silence was broken by a heavy knock.

Kaleigh set her glass down on the side table and shifted towards the door. "Did they forget something?"

"I don't think that knocking's from Miss Lewis." The second knock rattled the door's hinges. Jackson's stance was tense as he rose to check the peep hole. But his posture melted from protectiveness to fear when he saw who was behind the door. Marcus.

Jackson's hand felt thick and clumsy as he unlocked the doorknob and twisted it open. Then, he adopted a casual posture, leaning against the doorframe. "Dad. Thanks for the notice."

"If I'd have given it, would you have stuck around?" With no other greeting, Marcus pushed him aside and strode into the room like he owned it (which he did). His eyes landed on Kaleigh, unsurprised.

"I see you've been passing your time as usual."

Jackson straightened. "Now wait one minute. Kaleigh..."

Marcus turned on him and interjected, "I must have missed the change of address card. I had to go through our bank statements to find your apartment name. I don't like wasting time."

"I know you don't. So, why'd you come to see me?"

"In the hope that you'd be doing anything other than wasting your time with flings." Marcus and Jackson were dark, mirror images staring each other down, from their jet-black hair to their olive skin. The hockey star was no slouch when it came to physique, but Marcus was even bigger. His height helped him when he was intimidating his employees; as if he wasn't influential enough in his position, he had to have the physicality to back it up. Jackson hated that they looked alike.

"You're a sales associate, Jackson? With low performance reviews to boot? If you were in my region, I would have fired you by now."

"They should have some kind of employee confidentiality," Jackson muttered. Marcus must have pulled his Hydrangea employee records.

"I should have known something was up. You showed interest in working for the company. I humored your 'need for the shore' while you should have been working your way up in the central office. Only to find out that you've still been doing absolutely nothing. Hiding out in the stockroom like a teenage boy."

Marcus's finger stabbed down toward Jackson's chest, but years of fights had caused Jackson to stop reacting. He was now burrowed in the icy recesses of himself that kept his body frozen in place. Not able to respond, but also not easily broken.

Jackson's voice was cool. "It sounds like I've caused you a lot of embarrassment. But I may not always be here to boss around."

Marcus barked out a laugh. "Ooh. Going off on your own, huh? I should take you off the accounts, right now. Is that what you want?" He took his phone out, ready to make the call. Jackson remained rigid, all responses dead in his mouth. "No? That's what I thought. You wouldn't want to do any actual work." He shoved his phone back into his pocket. "You'd better get moving at that store of yours, or you're coming back home." He straightened, now the picture of civility, and nodded at Kaleigh. "Callie," he said, and stalked away.

To his left, Jackson saw Kaleigh's jaw drop, and to his right, Marcus slammed the door shut. Jackson chose to focus on the closed door. He didn't want to see Kaleigh looking at him like a weak, helpless loser.

It seemed a fitting metaphor for his life—doors kept closing, blocking out possibilities. Well, not anymore.

Marcus thought he knew everything, but he didn't know about Costa Rica. And Jackson wished he could stick around, just to see the look on his father's face the moment he realized that his son and his precious legacy was gone forever.

* * *

Marcus had looked Kaleigh up and down. She knew that look. Utter condescension, like she was the dirt beneath his feet. But she'd balled her fists and clamped her mouth shut, not wanting to give him any more ammunition to the words which implied she did not belong here. She didn't have to prove anything to the likes of him.

Jackson faced away from her, shoulders slumped, but he didn't have to be ashamed. He was not defined by his father. She hated when people lumped her and Lana together that way.

Still, Marcus's words squeezed like a steel trap around her heart. "Flings," he'd said. The word played right into her fears that she was just another girl to Jackson, being taken in by his charm only to be discarded when he grew bored.

But Jackson wasn't charming now. He just looked...broken. In a way that was painfully familiar to her. Maybe they both had their ways of acting fake, of telling the world that they didn't care what happened to them since the ones who should have loved them the most, didn't.

"You didn't deserve that," Kaleigh said.

"Neither did you. He shouldn't have spoken to you that way."

Kaleigh shrugged. "I'm no stranger to jerks."

"I guess you aren't." Jackson returned to the couch. He opened his mouth, then seemed to think better of it and snapped it shut.

"What is it?"

He shook his head. "No, it's none of my business."

Kaleigh crossed her arms. "Come on, spit it out."

"Was Aaron's father one of those jerks?" Jackson looked both curious and cautious.

"The biggest."

"He left you guys?"

"Yes. He wouldn't even stick around for the mother of his child. He was too gutless," she spat the word out like a curse, "to even try. I didn't want to be with him, really—I mean, it's not like he was such a winner. I'm angry more than anything."

Jackson's fingers brushed hers. "He's the one who's missing out." When she didn't pull away, he grasped her whole hand. "I wish he was around so I could take a swing at him."

"It wouldn't do any good." Kaleigh lifted one shoulder.

"It might for me."

Kaleigh smiled at that. It was nice to have someone sticking up for her for once. "I wanted Aaron to have a dad, but it's for the best. Aaron should have family that loves and appreciates him. Not someone who only loves him when it's convenient."

Jackson nodded his agreement.

Kaleigh usually avoided talking about Aaron's father, but now that Jackson'd tapped that bitter well, all the hatred came spewing out. "And you want to know why I don't believe in God? I've lived my entire life subject to every whim of my mother. Then, the boy who claimed to love me left at the first sign of trouble. I mean, if God's pulling the strings, how can He expect me to carry on like this? If I hadn't found you..." She trailed off.

There she went, depending on someone. But if she didn't believe in her heart that he would stay, if she kept her past in the forefront of her mind, maybe she could stay in control.

"But you did find me." Jackson took her other hand and leaned forward. "And you carried on, in whatever way you could. You'll always do that for Aaron. I just wish you could see that you don't have to do it all by yourself. I don't know much about the Bible, about being a good Christian, but I know that my life's gotten better since I've started to follow God. Not easier. Just, more satisfying." He stared at their intertwined fingers. "Filled with better blessings than I could have hoped to receive."

Kaleigh's voice fell to a whisper. "This feels too good to be real." *Oh, how I want it to be real.*

Jackson matched her hushed tone. "I'm here," he promised. They leaned closer until they heard the doorknob turn.

"Always interrupted," Jackson said, but as he leaned back and slid his fingers from hers, his grin let her know he wasn't frustrated. Her son wasn't a burden. He was a "blessing." They turned to face the door and put all the earlier unpleasantness behind them.

* * *

Dinner passed without another hitch, but the apartment seemed so empty once everyone went home. The quiet hummed, hemming Jackson in until he turned on the flat-screen in the bedroom to stay distracted.

As the football announcers blared, he slid into his pajama pants, turned off the light, and crawled into bed. Still, the familiar fear that he wouldn't be able to fall asleep plucked at his chest.

He snapped his eyes open, shut the game off, and used his phone to play one of those cheesy deep-breathing audio clips with the wind chimes and the birds chirping instead.

He didn't put on any covers because he could hear Duke's collar jingling as the dog trotted across the apartment. Once Duke turned the corner into Jackson's room, he jumped up and sidled next to Jackson in bed. Then, there was no need for additional warmth. When the feel of Duke's bristly fur and heavy breathing fused with the soft hum of the narrator's voice, Jackson faded into sleep.

Jackson punched the accelerator down, the pavement like his

racetrack until he saw the car he hadn't noticed before. His foot slammed the brake pedal to the floor, but the reaction was late, too late... As he hurtled closer, the other driver came into view.

Jackson's headlights glinted off her hair. But instead of being a pale blond color like in his usual nightmare, the driver's hair was a fiery red. Kaleigh's blue eyes widened just before Jackson's vehicle smashed into hers, crushing her in its destruction.

Jackson thrashed backwards, not into the headrest of his car, but into his pillow. The motion jarred him awake.

Duke whined, unhappy that Jackson disturbed his snooze, and leapt off the bed.

Jackson sat up and shook the sleep out of his arms, not wanting to risk a return to the nightmare.

Logically, he knew that his fear of hurting Kaleigh had mingled with his old memories of the accident. But the paralysis he felt was identical to that horrible day. He had been frozen—too afraid to make a move that would create more problems.

God, he prayed, running his fingers through his hair. *Please make it clear what I'm supposed to do. I don't know what's right anymore.*

Isaac's charge to not wait too long resounded in Jackson's mind, but he shoved the thought back down. *It's too soon to talk to Kaleigh. She won't understand.*

Visualizing how that conversation would go was almost worse than the thought of getting back behind the wheel.

Jackson's stomach churned as fast as his new stand mixer when he imagined the hurt and betrayal he'd witness in Kaleigh's eyes. Or worse, the same cool detachment he'd only recently gotten rid of.

The Costa Rica topic was not helping him relax. He would be a mess tomorrow if he kept this line of thinking going.

Jackson decided to push his earbuds in and go for a midnight run. Maybe he could run hard enough to escape the truth—he couldn't delay a fallout much longer.

12

Under the shelter of fresh daylight, Jackson was napping on the couch when a text buzzed through from Kaleigh:

Hey, I blew a tire. We're okay, we're on the side of Smith Street. If you can't come, no worries. The tow truck will be here in an hour.

Jackson stared down at his phone. It was D'Angelo's day off. He might come if Jackson asked him to, but the man deserved a break.

Kaleigh had willingly reached out to him with something that she needed. How could he let her down?

Jackson hopped off the sofa, put his slides on, and grabbed his keys. The touch of the fob made him gag.

He ignored the reflex and headed for the car, shoving down the urge to halt just outside the vehicle. He flung the door open and sat.

His shaking hands caused the other keys to jingle as he stuck the one in the ignition that would bring the engine to life. Jackson took a shuddering breath, and then rolled his shoulders before turning the fob and clutching the wheel with both hands.

He had to get himself under better control, or he wouldn't be able to safely steer. He closed his eyes as he forced the image of Kaleigh and Aaron on the side of the road into his mind.

He bet she was trying to keep Aaron distracted by telling him to count the cars that went by or encouraging him to imagine where each driver might be going. Kaleigh was creative like that. And she was waiting for him.

Determination creased his forehead, and he snapped his eyes open, shifting the car into reverse. As he pulled out of the apartment lot and onto the main drive for the first time, the sight of an oncoming car made him flinch.

"It's not going to hit you," he told himself. "You didn't die in that crash in June, and you are not going to die today." Had it always been this hard to keep the wheels within the lines?

Jackson flipped on the radio to distract himself from the sounds of the engine that he felt sure was about to explode. The trip wasn't so far. He could make it. He asked his car's voice-controlled assistant to text Kaleigh back, and to tell her that he was on his way.

* * *

Kaleigh was afraid to expect that Jackson would show. Though he'd proved himself to be reliable lately, she never had been able to squelch the sense that time spent waiting on anyone besides herself was a waste.

But there he was, in the driver's seat of that ridiculously luxurious green sportscar. Jackson parked beside where she and Aaron stood and threw his hazards on.

Through the passenger window, Kaleigh could see him blow out a breath and grin. He jumped out, sprinted to the curb, and threw his hands toward the car. "M'lady. Your chariot awaits."

"Thank you. I owe you again."

He leaned against the vehicle. "You don't owe me anything."

Kaleigh set to work finagling Aaron's booster into Jackson's tiny backseat. "You know," she said, "all of the times I've run into you at work, I've never seen you drive."

"You noticed that, huh?"

Kaleigh cast her eyes down, embarrassed now. "To be honest, I thought you might have never learned. I assumed it was another rich kid thing."

"Oh, I learned. And now, I've just re-learned." He shook his head in disbelief. "I should be thanking *you*."

Kaleigh wondered what he meant by re-learned. He was acting strange—ecstatic, even.

Then again, Jackson always seemed happy to help her out. He didn't ever remind her about all he was giving up to be there like her mom would have done, or push her to move faster than she wanted to like her ex would have done.

Aaron gave Jackson a tight hug before climbing into his booster and buckling up. Kaleigh was all too happy to climb in her own tripped-out passenger seat. It was nice, being together again.

"What's that?" Aaron asked from the backseat, pointing to a black book on the floor beside him.

"My friend Isaac just bought me my first Bible."

"What's a Bible?"

Kaleigh tensed. *Here we go,* she thought. She had been hoping to put off the religion talk until Aaron got older.

Jackson looked at Kaleigh, inviting her to take the lead.

"It's a book that people who believe in God read," she said at last.

"Does it have any good stories in it?" Aaron asked.

"It does," Jackson answered. "Some of the stories are easier to understand than others, but I've been learning about them at church."

Aaron leaned forward as much as his seatbelt would allow. "Can we go to church with Jackson, Mommy?" he asked.

"Uhh..." Kaleigh'd always believed that, if there was a God, He didn't care much about her. However, she didn't want to end up like her mother.

Lana had hated religion, telling Kaleigh that men used it to treat women however they wanted. When Kaleigh started asking Lana more questions after she heard people at school talking about God, Lana would become irate and forbid her to speak any more about it.

"If you want to, baby. I'm..."

"Off tomorrow," Jackson finished.

"Stalker," she muttered. She turned toward the window, resting her elbow against the armrest and her cheek against her fist. *Well, that's that,* she thought. *I guess I'm going to church.*

* * *

Sunday morning, Kaleigh slid into Jackson's passenger seat, again in awe of the polished wood trim and tripped-out stereo system. "Why can't you just drive a normal car?" she asked.

He revved the engine. "I like something with a little power behind it."

"This town has one highway that has a speed limit above 35."

His expression turned serious. "Before my accident, I would have told you that those signs don't apply to me. Not when you have a good enough lawyer." He shook his head. "A good lawyer wouldn't have helped my conscience if I had hurt the other driver. Physically, I mean. I did hurt her by messing up her car, taking up her time."

"Everyone makes mistakes."

"Some people make more mistakes than others. But I shouldn't regret what happened. I'm prouder of my life now than I was before the accident. And someone recently reminded me that it's never too late to change."

Kaleigh didn't know if she believed that, but she kept quiet because it was a nice thought.

The closer they got to the church, the more nervous she felt. They would know. They would figure out that Aaron was not a little brother, not a nephew, but her son. Her son she had when she was eighteen and unmarried.

She smoothed down her denim skirt and peppered her tone with gravel. "I'll try this once. But don't expect me to come back."

"That's fine. Don't worry. Everyone here is great."

They would be nice, to him. He didn't have his history on display for everyone. And if they were rude to Aaron, she would turn around and leave.

"Are you scared, Mommy?" Aaron, in his nicest t-shirt and jeans, was worried about her again.

"No, honey. We're just going someplace new today. It's good to try new things. Sometimes we might end up liking them."

Kaleigh didn't want Aaron to end up jaded like her, but then again, experience hadn't given her any choice. Maybe him growing mad at the world was inevitable. Especially when Kaleigh's actions didn't always match up with her optimistic words.

They pulled in at the same time as Ava and Pete. As they all exited their vehicles, Ava smiled. "Kaleigh, it's nice to see you again." She pulled a steaming casserole which smelled like spicy peppers and melted cheddar out of Pete's car's backseat, embodying perfection again.

"You too." Kaleigh took Aaron by the hand and turned on Jackson. "Were we supposed to bring something? You didn't say anything about lunch."

"I usually run out and get a pizza after service. Don't worry, you guys can come with me. I won't leave you alone with the wolves." Jackson laughed, but at Kaleigh's sour expression, he cleared his throat. "I was nervous my first time coming too."

"I'm not nervous," she shot back, striding into the building. She slowed in the lobby when she saw heads turn in her direction. Jackson put a hand on her back and guided her to the sanctuary.

"People are staring at me," she pointed out under her breath.

"It's because you're so beautiful," he whispered back.

Kaleigh didn't know what was wrong with her. She forgot to accuse him of using a line but instead felt grateful he was there. Plus, at this point, there was nowhere to run.

She looked up at the lofty stained-glass panels which decorated the windows in the hallway. The colorful depictions of a cradled lamb and a dove in flight were beautiful, but the foreign images only increased her sense that she didn't belong.

A well-dressed man with slicked-back white hair hurried their way. "I'm Pastor Thomas," he said, extending his hand. "I'm glad to see you this morning."

Or are you just glad to have a bigger crowd? Kaleigh questioned as they shook hands, but she simply said, "Kaleigh Taylor. This is my son, Aaron."

Pastor Thomas didn't miss a beat. He leaned down and gave Aaron a high-five. "Hey, little guy. I hope you like it here today."

Kaleigh didn't have time to process his lack of a judgmental attitude because a pair of petite arms wrapped around her from behind. "Kaleigh!"

She whipped around. *Oh yeah,* she thought. *Mariana goes here too.*

Kaleigh was beginning to get the impression that she was at a Hydrangea reunion rather than a church service. At least Ava and Mariana were always friendly to her.

"Hey," Kaleigh replied, as the sound of a capella singing floated through the hall.

Jackson led them all to the sanctuary and sat down next to a tall man with floppy black hair. The man leaned over and shook Kaleigh's hand. "Hey there. I'm Isaac Wilson," he whispered. "This is my wife, Jess." A woman with wild curls and a flawless dark complexion waved. "And my son, Noah."

Isaac handed Kaleigh his open songbook while Noah stood on shaky legs to face Aaron. The tyke seemed to be around a year old, and Aaron knelt down to play toy trains with him, looking delighted to be the big kid for once.

Kaleigh thanked Isaac for the book but passed it over to Jackson. She wanted to take everything in and was definitely not going to sing. Jackson started warbling and sounded terrible.

Then, Jess was polite enough to pass Kaleigh her own open hymnal. Kaleigh still didn't want to sing but decided to look down at the words on the page:

But one was out on the hills away,
    far off from the gates of gold—
    away on the mountains wild and bare,
    away from the tender Shepherd's care.

"Lord thou hast here thy ninety and nine;
    are they not enough for thee?"
    But the Shepherd made answer:
    "This of mine has wandered away from me,
    and although the road be rough and steep,
    I go to the desert to find my sheep."

Kaleigh looked up and considered the lyrics. The image of a man caring about his hurting animal and seeking it out was surprisingly sweet.

She tuned back in for the final line of the song, repeated by the congregation: "Rejoice! For the Lord brings back his own. Rejoice! For the Lord brings back his own."

It must be nice to be under that type of protection, Kaleigh thought.

The congregation moved on to other songs, filled with traditional symbolism of the cross and God's love. *They sure seem into what they're singing.*

Finally, Pastor Thomas stood, and the people fell silent. He stepped up to stand behind the wooden pulpit.

"Let us pray," he said, and their heads lowered. Kaleigh peeked at Aaron, but he was playing quietly as usual.

"I'm thankful, Lord, for the song service. We know that we too often wander away like the lost sheep in Your word, but you will always come to rescue us. We thank you for your grace. We know that we face many difficulties in the wilderness of this life, but you know each of us by name. You will never leave us, and you will never fail to call us back again. May we praise Your name today, for it is by Jesus that we can pray, Amen."

The dependable relationship explained in the pastor's prayer stoked the familiar longing for love in Kaleigh's heart, but it all sounded too good to be true. To have someone that watched over her, who would never take off or let her down? And if God truly knew her name, then why had he left her and Aaron alone all these years?

To her right, Noah squealed happily, and Isaac rubbed him gently on the shoulder. To her left, Jackson shifted and smiled as he caught her gaze.

In that moment, she could almost believe she and Aaron weren't alone after all.

The pastor spoke on how baptism was a picture of Christ's death, burial, and resurrection.

Behind him, a full tank of water gleamed behind a shiny pane of glass. Apparently, they would get to see a baptism after the message.

Great, Kaleigh thought. *I have to be here on a* special *Sunday*.

Despite everyone's friendliness, the longer she stayed, the faster Kaleigh bounced her left knee, feeling like her tolerance for new things was as full as that baptistry and about to brim over.

Eventually, the pastor stepped down from the pulpit and signaled for a woman in the front row to join him.

The woman was all beige, from her delicately-creased skin to her tan slacks and crinkled blouse. Even her shoulder-length, coiffed hair was a sandy blond. Only her bright blue eyes and rouged cheeks offered a touch of color.

Pastor Thomas asked the woman, "Is there anything you'd like to say?"

She took a step forward. Her voice was quiet, but steady, as she explained her feelings. "As many of you know, I've been away from the church for a long time. Not away from the belief, just away from the church. Sometimes I... I would sit there and argue with what the pastor had to say in my mind and I..." She clasped her hands together. "I would like to thank you all. I came here, and you made me feel so welcome. It felt like... like coming home." Her eyes and her voice lowered as she finished her speech.

Kaleigh peered at the congregation to inspect their reaction, but the tearful eyes of the rest of the church proved the speaker's insecurity unfounded.

Someone even shouted out, "We love you, sister," making Kaleigh jump.

A grateful smile grew on the woman's face. She and the pastor turned and parted ways, disappearing behind the twin doors placed on opposite sides of the baptistry.

Unity and enthusiasm filled the little church with light as if it were the heavenly hosts there celebrating instead of a ragtag gathering of untrained locals. Indeed, light did filter in from the large window behind the baptistry, highlighting the silhouettes of the men who worked together to unscrew the pulpit from its base and remove it, along with the other furniture on the sanctuary's platform, so that all could better see the baptistry behind.

One man took the lead, bending down in his three-piece suit and revealing the age spots on his shiny bald head. Another soon came to his rescue, a middle-aged hulk of a man with a black beard and kind eyes. Mariana's skinny seat partner—her boyfriend, no doubt—dragged away a dark wooden bench covered in green velvet cushions.

Finally, they'd unobstructed the view, and the woman and Pastor Thomas stepped down into the water, which lapped at their waists.

The pastor cupped one hand under her neck, supported her back with the other, and called, "I now baptize you in the name of the Father, and the Son, and the Holy Spirit. Amen."

He dunked her backward into the water with a smooth swoosh, and she resurfaced with a gasp and wide eyes. A second after, she grabbed her face and started to sob and smile all at the same time.

Pastor Thomas started singing "Amazing Grace," and the congregation joined him with spirit. Kaleigh'd heard the tired hymn before, at her grandmother's funeral and in movies, but this morning it sounded invigorated with new life.

Kaleigh wanted to support the woman's choice, though the practice was still unfamiliar to her. Her singing voice was nearly a whisper: "I once was lost, but now am found, was blind, but now I see."

"That girl went all the way under the water," Aaron recounted at full volume.

But no one hushed him or gave him a stern look. In fact, Kaleigh could see one lady chuckle. "Yes, that was pretty cool," she whispered.

Kaleigh had to find her songbook again since she didn't know the verses to "Amazing Grace," only the chorus. After the last verse, the "sister," as they called her, re-emerged and stood at the front of the church for a handshake.

When Kaleigh and Aaron's row walked up to greet her, the woman gave Kaleigh a full-on hug. It was strange, coming from someone she barely knew, but for once, Kaleigh wasn't wary of any ill-intent. Joy and openness seemed a common thing here.

They rounded the sanctuary back to their seats and Pastor Thomas closed the service in prayer, thanking God for their new member.

"Kaleigh!" Jess Wilson grabbed her hand as soon as the pastor spoke his last syllable. "I'm so glad to finally meet you! You guys should come over for Friday night pizza. Six o'clock."

Kaleigh nodded, a little stunned.

Jackson explained, "The Wilsons are kind enough to invite me to dinner from time to time. I'd be glad to take you and Aaron with me this weekend."

"Friday you're working the afternoon shift, remember? We'll only get there by six if we drive separately."

"Now who's memorizing people's schedules?" Jackson winked, and Kaleigh's mouth fell open.

Jess saved Kaleigh when she took her by the arm. "Stop monopolizing the visitor," she told Jackson.

She ushered Kaleigh, Noah, and Aaron in the direction of the lunchroom, asking Kaleigh to share all her tips on sleep and potty training.

"I'll get the pizza," Jackson mouthed as Kaleigh looked back to him. They exchanged a smile as Jess plowed ahead with her interrogation.

Kaleigh found she didn't mind getting spirited away. It was a nice surprise that people wanted to talk to her and that she could even provide expertise to someone. Church was shaping up to be better than Kaleigh expected.

13

Friday, when Isaac swung his front door open for Jackson, the Taylors were already in the living room chowing down on mozzarella sticks. Jackson noticed little Noah Wilson pulling on Aaron's arm, eager to gain his attention.

"Hey, man," Jackson shook Isaac's hand. "Need any help with the food?"

"Nah. I just have to take the pizzas out of the oven." Isaac held up his phone, which was illuminated with a five-minute countdown timer.

"What's this?" Jackson asked, sticking a thumb in the direction of a cardboard box that someone had shoved against the coat rack. The box was as tall as his chest.

"That's Jess's new shampoo bowl and chair. I wouldn't mention it if I were..."

"Yes, I'm getting around to opening it." Jess called out from beside Kaleigh on the couch. "Raising a child and starting a business at the same time isn't easy, Jackson!"

Jackson threw his hands up in the air. "Hey, no judgment here. I know starting a business is a huge undertaking."

Jess hopped to her feet. "Do you want to see my logo?"

"Yeah, she got the drawing part done fast enough," Isaac murmured.

Jess whacked her husband's shoulder as she ran into a side room and retrieved a blue plastic folder.

From the folder, she produced a brand sheet that featured "Wilson Designs" in cursive at the top, set aesthetically below a pair of scissors and two combs in a "W" shape.

Jackson scanned Jess's business plan. "This looks great. You've registered with the city?"

"Yep."

"And with the state board?"

"Uh-huh. We have to modify the entrance to our side room to bring it up to code, though." She rested her hands on Isaac's shoulders and gave him a kiss on the cheek. "It's a little messy now, but it will be great for the house's value, right, honey?"

"Yes, in the long run," he squeaked out through tight lips, evidently stressed at the current state of their home (and their finances).

Jackson asked Jess, "And you've applied for a tax number?"

"That's the next thing on my list." She cocked her head. "How do you know so much about this?"

Jackson shrugged. "Those four years of business school paid off." He left off a complaint about how much he'd hated the college classes, not wanting to draw attention to that fact when Kaleigh was throwing all her efforts behind gaining an acceptance letter.

"Business, huh? So, are you planning on working your way up at Hydrangea, or will you start something of your own?"

"To be honest, I'm not really sure what the future holds for me."

He caught Kaleigh watching him, but she quickly turned away.

He would need to decide what his future held, and soon.

* * *

Kaleigh was amazed at the warmth that permeated the Wilson home. When Noah dumped his entire basket of toys over, neither of his parents raised their voices at him. When Isaac passed by Jess, he never failed to gently brush her arm or the small of her back with his hand. The two were clearly still in love.

"How long have you been together?" Kaleigh asked.

"We've been married three years," Jess said. "But we started dating sophomore year of high school, so we've been together for six years."

"That's amazing." Lana's longest relationship had lasted a year, and what a nightmare that had been.

"My parents are celebrating their twenty-fifth anniversary, though. We still have a long way to go!"

"Jess, you made the rest of our marriage sound like a life sentence." Isaac laughed from the kitchen.

Kaleigh watched him pull the pizzas from the oven. "Well, I'm sure you'll be fine with such a great example ahead of you."

Isaac set the pizzas on the island and looked at Jackson, who was lingering nearby. "We're blessed to have Jess's parents as an example, but my parents couldn't make their relationship work. Some people think that if our parents are a certain way, we're destined to follow in their footsteps. But I say that it's a choice. I've seen people who are hurt by a family member turn out more determined than ever to do things right."

"We don't take anything for granted," Jess added, hugging a tasseled throw pillow to her middle. "We definitely need Jesus. But it's a beautiful experience, to grow with and get to know another person every day of the rest of your life."

"Yeah," Kaleigh said, as if she had any idea. She didn't expect to ever share in that experience. She'd be thrilled if she only could keep providing a stable home for Aaron.

After Isaac cut the pizza, Jess skipped over to get a salad out of the fridge—as if that could somehow counteract all the grease they were about to consume. Kaleigh ushered the two children into the kitchen where Isaac asked the blessing.

"Thank you, Lord, for the friends gathered here tonight. May our conversations and time together be to Your honor, in Jesus's name, Amen."

Kaleigh lifted her head, a strange warmth in her middle at being called a friend. It had been a while.

Though Kaleigh was a near-stranger with nothing to offer them, the Wilsons hadn't made her feel out of place. They had treated her with thoughtfulness and courtesy at every turn. She guessed that was how they treated everyone. Welcoming them, practicing what they preached...

That revelation was a little disorienting. First, Jackson was being reliable. Then, Jess, a church girl, was not only tolerating Aaron, but acted thrilled that their kids could play together. She could almost believe that their religion wasn't fake.

A small voice in her head told her, *God is with you in the good times and the bad*, but she swatted it away. She'd had enough bad times to last her a lifetime. It was time to start thinking positively, because things were finally starting to go right.

* * *

At dinner last night, Kaleigh'd shared with the table that she'd logged her fifth volunteer hour. Of course, Jackson had been the one watching Aaron, but he hadn't realized how many weeks had passed.

To celebrate the fact that she was now halfway done with her admission requirement, Jackson ordered Kaleigh a bouquet of daisies, all dyed in various, vivid colors.

In the past when he had ordered flowers for a girl, he had chosen long-stemmed roses or more expensive arrangements, but he felt like something simple and beautiful would match Kaleigh perfectly.

Monday morning, Jackson stood in Hydrangea's parking lot holding up the collection of blooms. He felt like an idiot until he saw Kaleigh's car drive up. She rolled her window down.

"What are those?" she asked, her eyes guarded.

"A congratulations, and I'm proud of you." He handed her the bouquet through the window.

She took it into her lap and stared down at the flowers for a moment. "Thank you. They're beautiful." She hadn't met his eyes, but her voice was soft. "Give me a second to park."

Jackson backtracked to the sidewalk to wait for her.

After a minute, Kaleigh joined him, crumpling the top of her sack lunch in her hands. "So, I guess you're almost off the hook for babysitting now."

"Am I?"

She nodded. "Thankfully, the PTA program is all online. Once I'm accepted, I'll be able to take my classes while Aaron is asleep."

"I know you're a hard worker, but that sounds like a lot. Maybe... I could still hang out with him sometimes? Just when you need to catch up on everything?"

Kaleigh met his eyes and took a step closer. "And why would you want to do that?"

"Don't you already know?" Jackson whispered. A strand of her silky red hair had escaped from her ponytail, and he ran it carefully between his fingers. He moved slowly, like a nature photographer not wanting to startle an exquisite butterfly.

She turned his face up to his, and that was all the encouragement Jackson needed. The desire of the past few weeks welled up inside him, and he kissed her like a starving man, losing himself in her sweet apple scent and satin lips.

She hadn't answered his question, but if Kaleigh didn't already know how much he cared about her, Jackson hoped this would clear things up.

The usually blocked-off Kaleigh was now a fireball of passion. Apparently, she'd been fighting back feelings of attraction as much as he had. All this time, Jackson had hoped that she liked him, but it was only now that he felt sure.

More cars pulled in and Kaleigh ended the kiss. It was a good thing, too, because Jackson never would have. He wanted to kiss her over, and over…

He took a deep breath and tilted his forehead to rest on hers, his thumb stroking her chin.

The bell of the store's entrance tinkled as Mariana swung the door open and called out, "Jackson!" She saw them together and halted, putting a hand over her mouth. "I'm so sorry. I'm interrupting again."

Jackson lifted his head but stayed close to Kaleigh. "What do you need?" His voice came out rough, and he cleared his throat.

"Jenny posted an application for a temp sales position and got lots of interest. It should be easy for her to hire someone to work on a short-term basis, if you decide to come back next year."

Kaleigh leapt away from Jackson like she had just grabbed the top of a barbed wire fence. "If you decide to come back next year? You're leaving? What is she talking about?"

Mariana backed away. "I can see this is a bad time. I'll catch you later, Jackson." She practically ran back into Hydrangea.

Kaleigh actually hit him on the arm. He stumbled back a step, though his limbs were slack with shock. "I said, what is she talking about?"

Jackson swallowed past the lump in his throat. "She's talking about my January term of service. I'm supposed to volunteer overseas with underprivileged youth in Costa Rica."

"Oh." Her face crumpled with hurt before she set it like stone.

"Listen, Kaleigh."

She shook her head and put her hand up. "It's okay. You don't owe me an explanation."

"I do, I—"

"No, you don't. I'm just a friend that you work with. You have every right to tell whatever *friends* you want about leaving the country." She stalked toward the store.

Jackson chased after her. "I haven't decided for sure if I'm going. This has been my dream for years, but now I'm confused—I'm not sure what I want."

Kaleigh nodded but kept walking, her face set forward. Jackson followed her into Hydrangea, still pleading, but she marched straight into the women's bathroom.

Right when Jackson had got Kaleigh to trust him, he could not have messed it up any more.

* * *

Kaleigh tried to silence the bells in her mind that kept clanging: stupid, stupid, stupid. Would she ever learn?

It seemed that Jackson had found time to tell both Jenny and Mariana that he was planning on leaving for a year. She didn't know why the topic hadn't come up in all of their recent conversations. Unless he was hiding information to protect himself, because he knew that she wouldn't like it. Unless their kiss hadn't meant half as much to Jackson as it'd meant to Kaleigh.

The next day, she went back to avoiding Jackson at work (politely, though, rather than with the heavy helping of hostility she had handed him after he'd let her down the first time). It was hard, though. She had grown used to having him around, and was surprised how much she missed the carefree teasing that she used to mock him for.

Maybe Kaleigh should have replied to Jackson's texts begging her to hear him out. Each one sounded more and more desperate until he sent his last:

I'm sorry. I've never been good at keeping a relationship, and I

shouldn't have tried with you. Just know I'll never regret meeting you and your wonderful son.

She didn't know why she kept reading the texts in bed after she'd put Aaron down for the night. The words only made her hands shake and her eyes water. Taking shallow breaths did little to fill the throbbing emptiness inside.

All her life, Kaleigh'd tried to build a rock-solid fortress around her heart, but Jackson shattered her supposed strength like it was made of shale.

Maybe Kaleigh owed Jackson a reply after everything he'd done for them, but she had to protect herself. This hurt too much, and she couldn't afford to fall apart. She'd thought Jackson loved her, but of course he didn't. No one did, except for Aaron.

The worst part was that Aaron asked her when they were going to see Jackson again. It would have been nice if she had been able to maintain one stable relationship with an adult. Instead, she had put Aaron in a situation where he had to make sense of all the fractured pieces.

Almost as if God had heard her plea for a lasting relationship, and decided to grant her a sick answer to it, a text came in from Lana:

I'm coming home.

Kaleigh couldn't move her finger to reply yet. The weight of her despair at the cycle restarting felt so heavy. In the stillness, she drifted off to sleep.

She dreamed of strong arms holding her. They weren't Jackson's arms—she didn't see anyone at all in the grassy, sunlit field. She only felt a gentle breeze and the sensation of being carried.

She looked down at the softest, most lovely violet dress she'd ever seen. It had cap sleeves and a sweetheart neckline. She was perfectly comfortable. Soft. Radiant. She felt like a small child, cared for, loved, and seen for who she really was. That was when she knew it was a dream.

Kaleigh opened her eyes and blinked away hot tears. Pain and suffering were her reality. Strength and silence. She would survive this, like she'd survived everything else.

* * *

She was freezing Jackson out. He would know—he'd done it enough to other people.

Oh, well. I don't need—his mind skipped over the name that was too painful to repeat, even silently.

He figured that he'd gotten by for twenty-three years on his own. He would go on to Costa Rica, to those who wanted his help, and pray that he didn't mess that up, too.

What other option did he have? Work at Hydrangea seeing—*her*—every day? Jackson had never intended to listen to irate parents or fetch tutus forever.

And what if his father bullied him into a corporate promotion? He couldn't see himself in some tomb of an office, doing the same thing every day for the next forty years.

Jackson rubbed his forehead in frustration. If Kaleigh could only wait for him for a year... *But then what?* Jackson thought. *No.*

She had figured out what he had tried to deny. He was too selfish to be accountable for two other people, and he didn't have the experience to be able to hold a family together.

He'd bought stuff for them, provided a babysitting service, but he hadn't managed to guard Kaleigh and her son from himself. He'd lied to her again, broken her heart again. He'd wanted to prove that there were people that wouldn't let her down, but he'd done the exact opposite.

A random, staccato thought interrupted his lament. *Do you believe in God?*

Yes, he believed. He'd keep trying to serve Him with his mess of a life.

Do you believe I make all things new?

Jackson'd heard plenty about forgiveness and redemption at church. But he'd slid right back into his old selfish, cowardly ways.

Could God's mercy be big enough to cover him?

Could Kaleigh's?

He knew the answer to the second question. He wouldn't bother Kaleigh again, or pressure her to take his sorry self back.

If, by some miracle, Kaleigh reached out, it would be of her own free will. Even if that meant losing her forever.

14

"Aaron, it's time to eat," Kaleigh called as she stirred pasta sauce into the spaghetti. Aaron bolted down the hallway and into a kitchen chair. She pulled out a scalding bag of green beans from the microwave with two fingers and dropped it on the counter.

She heard Lana's door creak open as well, but her mother never bolted anywhere. "Spaghetti again?" she drawled.

"It's healthy, cheap, and Aaron likes it," Kaleigh replied. Keeping the takeout bill under control was yet another perpetual argument between them.

"What's he doing?" Lana asked, pointing to Aaron at the table. He had leaned over the scratched-up surface, with his hands folded and his eyes closed.

Kaleigh brought Aaron his plate and heard him say, "and please keep Jackson here, because I love him. Amen."

Kaleigh put the spaghetti down and stroked his hair. "Try not to get your hopes up, angel. But if God listens to anyone, I'm sure it would be you." She planted a kiss on his temple, and turned back to the fridge to get him a juice box.

"Ridiculous," Lana hissed under her breath.

"Can I speak with you outside for a minute, Mom?" Kaleigh asked, her tone clipped. It was one thing to demean every word that came out of Kaleigh's mouth. She couldn't stand the thought of Lana killing Aaron's dreams.

Lana pranced outside, her arms crossed. When Kaleigh had shut the door, Lana asked, "What?"

"We're really glad you came back," Kaleigh started, though she wasn't so sure about that. "But please don't talk to Aaron that way. I don't want to discourage him from doing something he's excited about."

"You're setting him up for more discouragement, teaching him to believe in fairy tales."

"He's five years old."

Lana fluffed out her glossy black hair. "He's growing up."

Visions of how fast she had had to grow up flashed in red behind Kaleigh's eyes. "Not yet," she ground out.

"Don't get mad at me because you can't manage your own child. You're the one who had him at eighteen."

Kaleigh knew rationally that pointing out Lana's hypocrisy would get her nowhere, but sometimes she couldn't help herself. "You were a pregnant teenager too!"

"Yes, I was, and think about how much easier my life would have been if I didn't have you." Lana stabbed a finger in time to the last three words at Kaleigh's chest.

But words like that didn't hurt or shame Kaleigh anymore. Even though she wouldn't be seeing Jackson or any of his friends as much after his betrayal, their time together had made her realize that real love didn't talk like that.

Kaleigh could almost pity Lana, knowing that her mother was missing out on the closeness that Kaleigh and Aaron had. But that pity was not greater than the need to circumvent any more damage to her family. "I need you to leave," she said.

"What?"

Kaleigh pointed back to the apartment. "Please pack your things, and get out."

"You can't disrespect me like this," Lana spluttered. "And just think of Aaron."

"I am thinking of Aaron. You can stay for dinner, but then, please call your friends and see if there is somewhere else you can go."

"Ungrateful girl. Just see how far you can make it without me. You can't handle that little boy. Raising a child on your own is not as easy as I made it look, you'll see."

Kaleigh simply returned to the living room and doled out the rest of supper in silence.

Lana was right, it wouldn't be easy, but neither would Kaleigh continue to let the fear of letting people in stop her from getting help. Nice people were out there, and Kaleigh needed to surround herself with them. She could only hope that one day, Lana would see her daughter's example and do the same.

* * *

Kaleigh woke up feeling uneasy. She didn't know why. She didn't have to worry about Lana giving her a hard time anymore—last night, her mother had texted a friend and left before brownies.

Kaleigh glanced at her phone. It was eight a.m. Aaron usually woke her up by now.

She unplugged the phone and pulled an oversized sweatshirt over her pajamas. In her slippers, she padded over to Lana's old room, which Aaron had asked to move into last night. The bed was empty.

"Aaron?" she called, returning to the kitchen.

The open pantry door caught her eye, where a jumbo box of pre-bagged snack crackers was turned on its side. Aaron's backpack, which he loved to fill with his crayons and drawings, was missing from beside the kitchen table. Her wallet, on top of the table, was open.

"Aaron!" she cried. Her fingers tingled and vision fogged. She shook her head to clear it. She couldn't give in now. Her baby was missing.

Kaleigh ran outside, hoping he had just left, but saw no one. She called Lana.

Her mother answered coolly. "Are you asking me to come back already?"

"Did you take Aaron?"

"Really, Kaleigh, your outburst last night was enough. You don't have to accuse me of kidnapping my own grandson."

Kaleigh figured her mother was telling the truth. Lana wouldn't willingly take on that much responsibility, even to make Kaleigh mad, and she certainly wouldn't have had to make a mess of the junk food.

Lana's voice grew concerned. "He's probably just playing somewhere in the house."

"He isn't. He would have answered when I called."

"Check the park. And anywhere he could walk to that he likes to go."

"I'll let you know when I find him." Kaleigh hung up.

She grabbed her keys and ran to Mrs. McCauley's apartment first.

Her neighbor swung open the door after a few hard knocks. "Kaleigh. What's the matter?"

"Aaron's missing. Have you seen him today?"

Her mouth dropped open. "No. What can I do?"

Kaleigh took her house key off her key ring and placed it in Mrs. McCauley's wrinkled hand. "Stay in my apartment in case he comes back. I've got to keep looking."

Mrs. McCauley nodded and shuffled over to her end table to get her cell phone, but Kaleigh didn't have time to linger.

She raced to her car and sped to the community playground. She scanned the swings first, then got out and peered through all the bright yellow tunnels, but Aaron wasn't hiding in any of them.

The tears started falling as Kaleigh returned to her car. She rested her forehead on the steering wheel for a moment. Then, with trembling hands, she dialed 911.

A woman with a professional voice picked up immediately. "911, what's your emergency?"

"My child is missing," Kaleigh choked, the spoken words making it feel so much more real.

"When did you discover that he or she was missing?"

"This morning, when I woke up. I haven't seen him since I tucked him in last night. He's never done anything like this before."

"What is your son's name?"

"Aaron Taylor." She pulled at her messy bun. "He has dark blond hair, brown eyes, and he'll be five in two days."

"Height and weight?"

"Umm..." Why couldn't she think? "I'm not sure, but at doctor's appointments, he is usually in the fiftieth percentile for weight and ninetieth for height."

"Don't worry, ma'am, I can pull up a growth chart. Is there anyone who Aaron might be with? His father, maybe?"

"No, I haven't had contact with his father in five years."

"Where else could he have gone?"

Breathe in, breathe out. "I checked our playground. I'm not sure where else he could have gone on his own."

"Does Aaron know how to use public transportation?"

Kaleigh gripped the phone tighter. "We took the city bus to the hospital before, when I had car trouble. It looks like he took money out of my wallet."

"We'll send a team to the hospital, and also set up a perimeter around your neighborhood. Please keep your phone on you. We'll be by to collect a photograph."

Kaleigh nodded along in a daze before realizing the operator couldn't see her. "Of course. Thank you."

The operator broke the connection. Kaleigh's head was pounding. She couldn't just sit here. She needed backup.

Without a moment of hesitation, she called Jackson. Their relationship drama didn't matter anymore. He picked up on the third ring.

"Aaron's gone," Kaleigh wailed. "I don't know where he is!"

"Where are you?" Jackson asked.

"I'm at our neighborhood playground."

"I'll be right there, stay where you are."

Kaleigh numbly watched the minutes click by on the dashboard's digital display. In just two minute's time, Jackson pulled in the parking space to her left, his tires squealing.

He yanked open Kaleigh's door and gathered her into his arms. The embrace slowed Kaleigh's thundering pulse, but she couldn't linger there long.

"The 911 operator thought Aaron might've taken a bus. Let's check the library. He loves going to story time there. Wait —" Kaleigh's brain struggled to click thoughts together in the right order. "I need to leave a picture for the police. Run by my apartment first." They buckled up and took off in Jackson's car.

Back home, Kaleigh blew by Mrs. MacCauley in the living room, hollering that there'd been no news. She hurried to her bedroom, yanked a recent photo of Aaron out of an album, and offered it to the sitter. "Please give this to the police if we're not back before they come."

Mrs. MacCauley nodded.

The 911 operator had likely assumed Kaleigh would stay at the apartment and meet with the police, but Kaleigh never had been very good at sitting still. She had to do something for Aaron, or she'd go crazy.

Jackson'd never been to the town's library before, so Kaleigh fed him directions on the way. They soon arrived at the white, historical building a few blocks from the downtown area.

Jackson questioned the librarian at the front desk while Kaleigh ran through the library's three small rooms, but Aaron was nowhere to be found.

"What about the store?" Jackson asked.

"I do grocery delivery. We never go anywhere else." Kaleigh massaged her temples.

Jackson thought for a moment. "I'll text Pastor Thomas and tell him to get the members to start looking, too, starting with the church building."

"Let's go to the church too. I have to keep searching, I can't just wait around."

Jackson nodded, and they zoomed off again.

When they drove up, the tall house of worship loomed like a prison rather than a haven. *If he isn't here...*

Kaleigh staggered up the stairs where Pastor Thomas was unlocking the front door. She burst through as soon as he pulled the door open.

"Aaron?" Her voice echoed forlornly through the empty building. Jackson took a left, so she went right towards the sanctuary.

Kaleigh didn't know where the light switches were, but enough sun was coming through the stained glass that it didn't matter. The air must have been turned off, and the heat felt oppressive as she stalked down the rows of chairs in the open room.

She crouched on her knees to look underneath the chairs once she reached the front.

Combing through yet another place where Aaron was absent stripped Kaleigh of all her energy. She sat back on her heels and looked up at the pulpit.

"God, are you here?" she whispered.

She had tried her best to do right by Aaron, and still she had lost him. After all her years of struggling and loving, he was gone.

"God, I will never ask for anything again. Please, please bring him back." Her tears streamed down. "I have to see him again."

Kaleigh remembered how scared she had been when she found out she was pregnant. Even when he was old enough to move in her belly, the sensation felt alien as the unexpected little guy turned her world (and her stomach) upside down for nine months. But when the nurses had placed Aaron on her chest the moment after he was born, and he quieted like he knew her, joy and purpose had flooded through all of her doubts.

Looking back, Kaleigh regretted deeply every time she had been resentful for having no time for herself. She was sorry for any moment that she wasted being stressed out and frustrated with Aaron. She lowered her head back to the ground, still whispering, "Please. Please."

No mystical voice descended from the heavens and revealed the location of her son. But two, short, impossible phrases echoed in her mind. *I have you. I'm here.*

Some time later, she felt Jackson's large hand on her shoulder. She hadn't even heard him come in.

"I didn't find him," he said, his voice strained. "I was thinking, maybe we should check Johnson's Family Farm? I know he went there once, for the fall festival."

Kaleigh slowly rose and swiped her cheeks. "I'll try anything."

Jackson took her by the hand as her determination had morphed into a fog, as if she was out of her body.

They got in the car and drove out of town, down the country road that led out to the sprawling ranch. Gravel crunched beneath Jackson's tires as they approached the red barn.

"Jackson," Kaleigh breathed, pointing through the windshield. A little figure was sitting on a haystack outside of the farm, bawling his eyes out.

Before Jackson had fully parked, Kaleigh flung open the door, rushed over, and swept her son up into her arms. "Aaron! Don't you ever do that to me again. I love you, I love you so much. What were you thinking?"

"I'm sorry, Mommy," Aaron cried, and Kaleigh shushed him, wiping the tears off of his face.

"I've got you now." She rocked him back and forth silently, giving him a moment to catch his breath.

When Aaron calmed down, he said, "I heard Grandma say your life would be easier if I left. I remembered that movie I watched at Jackson's house, where the little girl lied to the bus driver about where her mommy was, and made him drop her off at her favorite place. This is my favorite place, but it's scary without you."

"Of course it is, baby. And don't ever think that you make my life harder. You make my life worth living. You're the best thing that ever happened to me."

Aaron nodded and buried his face in her stomach.

Jackson stood by their side, tears in his eyes as well. Kaleigh waved him over so that he could sit on the haystack with them and put his arms around them both.

"I'm not going to Costa Rica," he burst out. "I don't care if you never speak to me again. I'm going to stay right here, where the people I love the most are. I will be here for you, in whatever way you need me. I love you," he repeated, breaking down into a sob.

Jackson'd been wrong to keep his plans from Kaleigh. But he'd also shown up for her and Aaron more times than she could count. His offering, his raw commitment gave her the courage to speak the truth that she'd been denying. She could make it without Jackson, but she no longer wanted to.

"We love you too."

Jackson pulled back, and—after searching for the confirmation in her eyes—his drawn, anxious face brightened with joy. He hugged them even harder, kissing the top of Kaleigh's head first, and then the top of Aaron's.

Aaron yelled out, "Finally."

Kaleigh knew she should probably reprimand Aaron for celebrating after scaring them to death, but she was so grateful he was there that she broke down into laughter instead.

After they called law enforcement, Pastor Thomas, Lana, and Mrs. McCauley, this would all be over. And they were going to be okay.

Epilogue

One Year Later

Jackson winked at Kaleigh on his way out of Hydrangea. He had worked the opening shift this morning, and Kaleigh would close the store down. He still couldn't believe that that resilient, gorgeous woman was his girl.

He drove to the parent pickup line at Citrus Ridge Elementary, where a very happy kindergartener rushed into his backseat, eager to tell Jackson all about the letter sounds he'd learned in school.

Jackson had always seen staying at Hydrangea as a death sentence, but now, it was a much happier place—a means to making all of their goals a reality.

In the mornings, Kaleigh took PTA classes, and on Jackson's days off, he poured all of his time into a newfound passion: creating a nonprofit.

Once the organization opened—with the newly-minted couple D'Angelo and Miss Lewis at its helm—single parents would be able to take parenting classes, earn incentives for life milestones like opening a savings account, receive childcare as often as once per week, and get career counseling. If it was up to Jackson, no one would have to struggle alone for years like Kaleigh had.

Bright Tomorrows was set to open in a month, and Jackson already had several donors from the community lined up to support the project. The biggest contributor of all, however, was Mr. Marcus Green of Iowa City.

The day he'd decided to face his father, Jackson'd called Marcus like a man. The question was too important to be texted or emailed.

Jackson had drummed his fingers against his couch's arm until Marcus picked up.

"Jackson?"

"Hi, Dad." He got straight to it. "I'm calling because I have a business proposal."

"I'm listening."

Jackson took a deep breath. "You've always told me to identify the consumer's need. Well, there is a great need to help single parents in this community."

Marcus's tone was droll. "And how do you intend to make a profit off of struggling parents?"

"I won't make a profit. But I was hoping that you might be interested in expanding your philanthropic interests. I have a contact who started a food pantry from the ground up, and she's willing to help me organize fundraisers to keep this thing going for the long run. We just need donors to get started."

Silence followed. It was not Marcus's usual style. "I can't say that I'm happy about this, Jackson," he finally said. "I wanted more for you than directing a charity and barely scraping by. Are you prepared to sacrifice your way of life?"

"Living for others isn't really a sacrifice. I think it's the best way to live." Jackson smiled. At last, he understood what Isaac, what *God* had been trying to teach him. "If you could keep funding my apartment for a few more months while I build a basic salary into the budget, I'll become independent."

"I'm glad you're showing some initiative. A philanthropic angle could help my case in making company VP."

Jackson held his breath. "Yes, it could."

"I'll have my secretary make the arrangements." Jackson could imagine Marcus's brisk nod from over the phone.

"Thank you, Father."

Marcus cleared his throat. "Goodbye, Jackson." He disconnected the call.

It hadn't been easy to call him father, to remove all the angry names Jackson had attached to the man over twenty-three years from his mind.

As Jackson'd made mistakes and been forgiven by Kaleigh, and by God, he had to work to let go of this past pain.

The memories still visited Jackson often. The vision of his driver in the bleachers during his first hockey game, instead of his father.

The anger he'd felt at Marcus's Christmas office party, witnessing big happy families singing carols and drinking punch, with siblings chasing each other around the tree.

Jackson's own upbringing had been stale and colorless. But that wasn't where he was now. He wanted to be grateful for new things, for good things. And to move forward in freedom toward the next chapter of his life, Jackson wouldn't be held prisoner by his dark days anymore.

* * *

On Tuesday mornings when Kaleigh wasn't scheduled to work, she and Aaron would meet Jess and Noah at the Summer Shores Community Center for an arts and crafts class. Aaron wasn't uppity about spending time with a boy who was three years younger than him. Instead, he'd adopted the toddler like a little brother and was now helping him to color, cut, and string ribbon through a paper lion mask.

Sitting with her friend, Kaleigh felt like she'd been adopted too, into a support system. She hadn't known how wonderful it would be to have another woman there who knew what she was going through. A woman who knew how to listen and give, instead of to twist and take.

As their children compared their masterpieces, Jess leaned over to Kaleigh and teased, "You and Jackson look like you're getting serious. He always has his arm around you in church, and I've seen him grab your hand under the lunch table."

Jackson had been the perfect gentleman at the beginning of their official relationship, so much so that Kaleigh'd started to complain. Now, they were nearly inseparable. "He asked me what I thought about marriage the other day," she admitted.

"No."

"Yes. I said that I never thought I would get married. But my whole life has turned out differently than I'd thought, in the best way. I trust him, and I don't want to be with anyone else. So... why not?"

"Does this mean you're engaged?" Jess's voice squeaked, and Kaleigh shushed her.

"No. We were just talking."

"Still, he could propose any day now!" Jess threw her arms around Kaleigh. "I'm so happy for you."

It was all a little overwhelming. But the truth was, "I'm happy, too."

* * *

Kaleigh and Aaron kept going to church after their initial visit, their connection to the teaching and the members growing until both had asked to be baptized.

Jackson had thought that the fall festival was his happiest day. And, later, when he and Kaleigh had gone on their first official date.

But seeing the little boy he loved more than life rise up out of that water, grinning from ear to ear—seeing Kaleigh laugh like an unburdened child herself—his days just kept getting better.

Truly, God had redeemed the hard times the Taylors had experienced, and, through them, He had redeemed Jackson from his loneliness. God had even saved him from his doubting when he almost let his best gifts go.

Though Jackson knew he was unworthy of all he had been given, he was grateful. And thinking about all that had transpired gave Jackson the courage to ask one more, very important question.

As he pulled out of the grade school parking lot, he looked to Aaron in the rearview mirror and asked, "How would you feel if I asked your mom to marry me?"

"Yeah! Whoo-hoo!" Aaron kicking the back of the driver's seat in celebration was all the answer Jackson needed. As he turned his gaze to the road, a smile broke free.

* * *

Kaleigh and Aaron met Jackson at the rink for what they thought was a normal skating lesson. He hadn't told Aaron when he would propose, too afraid that the little man couldn't keep a secret.

"Are you feeling okay?" Kaleigh asked as the boys put on their skates. She must have noticed Jackson's heavy breathing and the sheen of sweat on his brow.

"I'm just anxious to get out there," he hedged. It was the truth. Just not for the reasons Kaleigh was thinking. "Are you ready for your lesson, buddy?"

"Yep!"

After a year's worth of skating, Aaron was now able to gear up with only a minimal amount of help. Soon, Kaleigh settled into the bleachers while they took the ice.

"I've got a special warm-up exercise today," Jackson told Aaron. But instead of drawing wavy lines and X's on the ice to help Aaron practice rapid turns and crossovers, Jackson used his thick black marker to inscribe foot-long letters onto the surface, spelling out, "Will You Marry Me?"

Kaleigh watched him curiously, especially when Aaron started jumping up and down and waving at her, but from her seat in the bottom row, she hadn't read the words. By now, some of the other skaters had stopped to watch.

Jackson took Aaron—whose anticipation was rapidly transforming into a safety hazard—by the hand. They skated to the ice's entrance.

Kaleigh joined them. "What's going on?" Then she saw the words.

Jackson got down on one knee then, pulling the ring box from the pocket of his black windbreaker. The wet seeping through the knee of his jeans distracted him momentarily from his nerves enough to spit out what he needed to say.

"Kaleigh." He stared into her wide eyes. "For the first time in my life, I love someone much more than I love myself. You and Aaron mean more to me than anything on this earth. Will you marry me?"

"Get up." Kaleigh yanked Jackson to his feet. It wasn't the answer he was hoping for. Then, she jumped into his arms.

His skates grasped for purchase, to no avail. For the second time this year, Kaleigh literally knocked him off his feet.

She grabbed his collar and pulled him in for an urgent kiss. Heat rushed through his body. He was surprised the ice wasn't steaming underneath him as he returned the kiss and clutched her closer. She'd said yes, she'd be his, forever.

The onlookers burst into applause and cheers. Jackson broke the kiss and chuckled. He eased Kaleigh to her feet and plucked up the engagement ring, which she'd knocked out of his hand in her eager acceptance. "Did you want this, or..."

"Yes!" Tears pooled behind Kaleigh's eyes as she took in the classic twist of diamonds. It was unfussy and exquisite, just like her. "It's beautiful. Thank you."

"You never have to thank me again. I'll spend every day trying to thank you for being the greatest gift of my life. You deserve the best, but I'm selfishly glad you've settled for me."

"You are the best." And as Kaleigh clutched his arms, she could almost make him believe it. He knew he hadn't earned a life with her and Aaron, their newly-shared faith, or a mending relationship with his parents. But he wasn't running from his failures anymore. He'd root himself deep down in love, in gratitude, living out the life God had perfectly portioned for them.

Psalm 68:5-6 "A father of the fatherless, and a judge of the widows, is God in his holy habitation. God setteth the solitary in families..."

THE END

Acknowledgements

All glory goes to God, for being so unconditionally good to me. This year He taught me that simply to see Him is a greater blessing than any of my plans.

I hope I will always use where I've been and where I'm at to help others. Writing isn't always easy, but I've grown a lot, and I'm excited to see what's next!

Thank you Tori and Ashley, for answering all of my technical questions.

To my number one fans Mom and Dad, for diligently reviewing pages.

To Savanna, Michaela, Sara, Emily, Robin, Kyla, and my writer's group for the story advice and encouragement! I also really appreciate all those who talked about the book and made me feel like I needed to keep going.

Thanks to Sofie for bringing this gorgeous cover to life, and Ben for always calling the Ninety and Nine hymn at church!

Much credit goes to Bob for putting up with my random gushing or venting sessions as I worked through the story, and to my children for being so inspirational.

I count myself fortunate to have such an incredible village behind me. May everyone that has a village be thankful for it, and may anyone who doesn't know that they are loved and not forgotten. Blessings!

About the Author

Rachel Blanchard is a teacher, wife, and mother of three young children. She received her Bachelor of Arts in English at Truman State University in Kirksville, Missouri before moving to Central Florida. She is passionate about sharing lessons learned, and the message that we can trust in God's goodness. If you enjoyed this story, please connect with Rachel at www.rachelblanchardwriter.com, or leave a review!

www.ingramcontent.com/pod-product-compliance
Lightning Source LLC
Chambersburg PA
CBHW030545130626
46552CB00006B/2437